# Sowing and Reaping

# Sowing and Reaping

Frances Ellen Watkins Harper

MINT EDITIONS

*Sowing and Reaping* was first published in 1876.

This edition published by Mint Editions 2020.

ISBN 9781513280165 | E-ISBN 9781513285184

Published by Mint Editions®

 MINT
EDITIONS

minteditionbooks.com

Publishing Director: Jennifer Newens
Design & Production: Rachel Lopez Metzger
Project Manager: Micaela Clark
Typesetting: Westchester Publishing Services

# Contents

# I

"I hear that John Andrews has given up his saloon; and a foolish thing it was. He was doing a splendid business. What could have induced him?"

"They say that his wife was bitterly opposed to the business. I don't know, but I think it quite likely. She has never seemed happy since John has kept saloon."

"Well, I would never let any woman lead me by the nose. I would let her know that as the living comes by me, the way of getting it is my affair, not hers, as long as she is well provided for."

"All men are not alike, and I confess that I value the peace and happiness of my home more than anything else; and I would not like to engage in any business which I knew was a source of constant pain to my wife."

"But, what right has a woman to complain, if she has every thing she wants. I would let her know pretty soon who holds the reins, if I had such an unreasonable creature to deal with. I think as much of my wife as any man, but I want her to know her place, and I know mine."

"What do you call her place?"

"I call her place staying at home and attending to her own affairs. Were I a laboring man I would never want my wife to take in work. When a woman has too much on hand, something has to be neglected. Now I always furnish my wife with sufficient help and supply every want but how I get the living, and where I go, and what company I keep, is my own business, and I would not allow the best woman in the world to interfere. I have often heard women say that they did not care what their husbands did, so that they provided for them; and I think such conclusions are very sensible."

"Well, John, I do not think so. I think a woman must be very selfish, if all she cares for her husband is, to have a good provider. I think her husband's honor and welfare should be as dear to her as her own; and no true woman and wife can be indifferent to the moral welfare of her husband. Neither man nor woman can live by bread alone in the highest and best sense of the term."

"Now Paul, don't go to preaching. You have always got some moon struck theories, some wild, visionary and impracticable ideas, which would work first rate, if men were angels and earth a paradise. Now don't be so serious, old fellow; but you know on this religion business, you and I always part company. You are always up in the clouds, while I am trying to invest in a few acres, or town lots of solid *terra firma*."

"And would your hold on earthly possessions, be less firm because you looked beyond the seen to the unseen?"

"I think it would, if I let conscience interfere constantly, with every business transaction I undertook. Now last week you lost $500 fair and square, because you would not foreclose that mortgage on Smith's property. I told you that 'business is business,' and that while I pitied the poor man, I would not have risked my money that way, but you said that conscience would not let you; that while other creditors were gathering like hungry vultures around the poor man, you would not join with them, and that you did not believe in striking a man when he is down. Now Paul, as a business man, if you want to succeed, you have got to look at business in a practical, common sense way. Smith is dead, and where is your money now?"

"Apparently lost; but the time may come when I shall feel that it was one of the best investments I ever made. Stranger things than that have happened. I confess that I felt the loss and it has somewhat cramped my business. Yet if it was to do over again, I don't think that I would act differently, and when I believe that Smith's death was hurried on by anxiety and business troubles, while I regret the loss of my money, I am thankful that I did not press my claim."

"Sour grapes, but you are right to put the best face on matters."

"No, if it were to do over again, I never would push a struggling man to the wall when he was making a desperate fight for his wife and little ones."

"Well! Paul, we are both young men just commencing life, and my motto is to look out for Number 1, and you—"

"Oh! I believe in lending a helping hand."

"So do I, when I can make every corner out to my advantage. I believe in every man looking out for himself."

You will see by the dialogue, that the characters I here introduce are the antipodes of each other. They had both been pupils in the same school, and in after life, being engaged as grocers, they frequently met and renewed their acquaintance. They were both established in business, having passed the threshold of that important event, "Setting out in life." As far as their outward life was concerned, they were acquaintances; but to each other's inner life they were strangers. John Anderson has a fine robust constitution, good intellectual abilities, and superior business faculties. He is eager, keen and alert, and if there is one article of faith that moulds and colors all his life more than anything else, it is a firm and unfaltering belief in the "main chance." He has made up his mind to be rich, and his highest ideal of existence may be expressed in four words—*getting on in life*. To this object, he is ready to sacrifice time, talent, energy and every faculty, which he possesses. Nay, he will go farther; he will spend honor, conscience and manhood, in an eager search for gold. He will change his heart into a ledger on which he will write *tare* and *tret*, loss and gain, exchange and barter, and he will succeed, as worldly men count success. He will add house to house; he will encompass the means of luxury; his purse will be plethoric but, oh, how poverty stricken his soul will be. Costly viands will please his taste, but unappeased hunger will gnaw at his soul. Amid the blasts of winter he will have the warmth of Calcutta in his home; and the health of the ocean and the breezes of the mountains shall fan his brow, amid the heats of summer, but there will be a coolness in his soul that no breath of summer can ever dispel; a fever in his spirit that no frozen confection can ever allay; he shall be rich in lands and houses, but fear of loss and a sense of poverty will poison the fountains of his life; and unless he repent, he shall go out into the eternities a pauper and a bankrupt.

Paul Clifford, whom we have also introduced to you, was the only son of a widow, whose young life had been overshadowed by the curse of intemperance. Her husband, a man of splendid abilities and magnificent culture, had fallen a victim to the wine cup. With true womanly devotion she had clung to him in the darkest hours, until death had broken his hold in life, and he was laid away the wreck of his former self in a drunkard's grave. Gathering up the remains of what had been an ample fortune, she installed herself in an humble and unpretending home in the suburbs of the city of B., and there with loving solicitude she had watched over and superintended the education of her only son. He was a promising boy, full of life and vivacity, having inherited much of the careless joyousness of his father's temperament; and although he was the light and joy of his home, yet his mother sometimes felt as if her heart was contracting with a spasm of agony, when she remembered that it was through that same geniality of disposition and wonderful fascination of manner, the tempter had woven his meshes for her husband, and that the qualities that made him so desirable at home, made him equally so to his jovial, careless, inexperienced companions. Fearful that the appetite for strong drink might have been transmitted to her child as a fatal legacy of sin, she sedulously endeavored to develop within him self control, feeling that the lack of it is a prolific cause of misery and crime, and she spared no pains to create within his mind a horror of intemperance, and when he was old enough to understand the nature of a vow, she knelt with him in earnest prayer, and pledging him to eternal enmity against everything that would intoxicate, whether fermented or distilled. In the morning she sowed the seed which she hoped would blossom in time, and bear fruit throughout eternity.

## II

## The Decision

I hear Belle," said Jeanette Roland addressing her cousin Belle Gordon, "that you have refused an excellent offer of marriage."

"Who said so?"

"Aunt Emma."

"I am very sorry that Ma told you, I think such things should be kept sacred from comment, and I think the woman is wanting in refinement and delicacy of feeling who makes the rejection of a lover a theme for conversation."

"Now you dear little prude I had no idea that you would take it so seriously but Aunt Emma was so disappointed and spoke of the rejected suitor in such glowing terms, and said that you had sacrificed a splendid opportunity because of some squeamish notions on the subject of temperance, and so of course, my dear cousin, it was just like me to let my curiosity overstep the bounds of prudence, and inquire why you rejected Mr. Romaine."

"Because I could not trust him."

"Couldn't trust him? Why Belle you are a greater enigma than ever. Why not?"

"Because I feel that the hands of a moderate drinker are not steady enough to hold my future happiness."

"Was that all? Why I breathe again, we girls would have to refuse almost every young man in our set, were we to take that stand."

"And suppose you were, would that be any greater misfortune than to be the wives of drunkards."

"I don't see the least danger. Ma has wine at her entertainments, and I have often handed it to young gentlemen, and I don't see the least harm in it. On last New Year's day we had more than fifty callers. Ma and I handed wine, to every one of them." "Oh I do wish people would abandon that pernicious custom of handing around wine on New Year's day. I do think it is a dangerous and reprehensible thing."

"Wherein lies the danger? Of course I do not approve of young men drinking in bar rooms and saloons, but I cannot see any harm in handing round wine at social gatherings. Not to do so would seem so odd."

"It is said Jeanette, 'He is a slave who does not be, in the right with two or three.' It is better, wiser far to stand alone in our integrity than to join with the multitude in doing wrong. You say while you do not approve of young men drinking in bar rooms and saloons, that you have no objection to their drinking beneath the shadow of their homes, why do you object to their drinking in saloons, and bar rooms?"

"Because it is vulgar. Oh! I think these bar rooms are horrid places. I would walk squares out of my way to keep from passing them." "And I object to intemperance not simply because I think it is vulgar but because I know it is wicked; and Jeanette I have a young brother for whose welfare I am constantly trembling; but I am not afraid that he will take his first glass of wine in a fashionable saloon, or flashy gin palace, but I do dread his entrance into what you call 'our set.' I fear that my brother has received as an inheritance a temperament which will be easily excited by stimulants, that an appetite for liquor once a awakened will be hard to subdue, and I am so fearful, that at some social gathering, a thoughtless girl will hand him a glass of wine, and that the first glass will be like adding fuel to a smouldering fire."

"Oh Belle do stop, what a train of horrors you can conjure out of an innocent glass of wine."

"Anything can be innocent that sparkles to betray, that charms at first, but later will bite like an adder and sting like a serpent."

"Really! Belle, if you keep on at this rate you will be a monomaniac on the temperance question. However I do not think Mr. Romaine will feel highly complimented to know that you refused him because you dreaded he might become a drunkard. You surely did not tell him so."

"Yes I did, and I do not think that I would have been a true friend to him, had I not done so."

"Oh! Belle, I never could have had the courage to have told him so."

"Why not?"

"I would have dreaded hurting his feelings. Were you not afraid of offending him?"

"I certainly shrank from the pain which I knew I must inflict, but because I valued his welfare more than my own feelings, I was constrained to be faithful to him. I told him that he was drifting where he ought steer, that instead of holding the helm and rudder of his young life, he was floating down the stream, and unless he stood firmly on the side of temperance, that I never would clasp hands will him for life."

"But Belle, perhaps you have done him more harm than good; may be you could have effected his reformation by consenting to marrying him."

"Jeanette, were I the wife of a drunken man I do not think there is any depth of degradation that I would not fathom with my love and pity in trying to save him. I believe I would cling to him, if even his own mother shrank from him. But I never would consent to marry any man, whom I knew to be unsteady in his principles and a moderate drinker. If his love for me and respect for himself were not strong enough to reform him before marriage, I should despair of effecting it afterwards, and with me in such a case discretion would be the better part of valor."

"And so you have given Mr. Romaine a release?"

"Yes, he is free."

"And I think you have thrown away a splendid opportunity."

"I don't think so, the risk was too perilous. Oh Jeanette, I know by mournful and bitter experience what it means to dwell beneath the shadow of a home cursed by intemperance. I know what it is to see that shadow deepen into the darkness of a drunkard's grave, and I dare not run the fearful risk."

"And yet Belle this has cost you a great deal, I can see it in the wanness of your face, in your eyes which in spite of yourself, are filled with sudden tears, I know from the intonations of your voice that you are suffering intensely."

"Yes Jeanette, I confess, it was like tearing up the roots of my life to look at this question fairly and squarely in the face, and to say, no; but I must learn to suffer and be strong, I am deeply pained, it is true, but I do not regret the steps I have taken. The man who claims my love and allegiance, must be a victor and not a slave. The reeling brain of a drunkard is not a safe foundation on which to build up a new home."

"Well Belle, you may be right, but I think I would have risked it. I don't think because Mr. Romaine drinks occasionally that I would have given him up. Oh young men will sow their wild oats."

"And as we sow, so must we reap, and as to saying about young men sowing their wild oats, I think it is full of pernicious license. A young man has no more right to sow his wild oats than a young woman. God never made one code of ethics for a man and another for a woman. And it is the duty of all true women to demand of men the same standard of morality that they do of woman."

"Ah Belle that is very fine in theory, but you would find it rather difficult, if you tried to reduce your theory to practice."

"All that may be true, but the difficulty of a duty is not a valid excuse for its non performance."

"My dear cousin it is not my role to be a reformer. I take things as I find them and drift along the tide of circumstances."

"And is that your highest ideal of life? Why Jeanette such a life is not worth living."

"Whether it is or not, I am living it and I rather enjoy it. Your vexing problems of life never disturb me. I do not think I am called to turn this great world 'right side up with care,' and so I float along singing as I go,

> *"I'd be a butterfly born in a bower*
> *Kissing every rose that is pleasant and sweet,*
> *I'd never languish for wealth or for power*
> *I'd never sigh to have slaves at my feet."*

"Such a life would never suit me, life must mean to me more than ease, luxury and indulgence, it must mean aspiration and consecration, endeavor and achievement."

"Well, Belle, should we live twenty years longer, I would like to meet you and see by comparing notes which of us shall have gathered the most sunshine or shadow from life."

"Yes Jeanette we will meet in less than twenty years, but before then your glad light eyes will be dim with tears, and the easy path you have striven to walk will be thickly strewn with thorn; and whether you deserve it or not, life will have for you a mournful earnestness, but notwithstanding all your frivolity and flippancy there is fine gold in your character, which the fire of affliction only will reveal."

# III

(Text missing.)

# IV

How is business?"

"Very dull, I am losing terribly."

"Any prospect of times brightening?"

"I don't see my way out clear; but I hope there will be a change for the better. Confidence has been greatly shaken, men of business have grown exceedingly timid about investing and there is a general depression in every department of trade and business."

"Now Paul will you listen to reason and common sense? I have a proposition to make. I am about to embark in a profitable business, and I know that it will pay better than anything else I could undertake in these times. Men will buy liquor if they have not got money for other things. I am going to open a first class saloon, and club-house, on M. Street, and if you will join with me we can make a splendid thing of it. Why just see how well off Joe Harden is since he set up in the business; and what airs he does put on! I know when he was not worth fifty dollars, and kept a little low groggery on the corner of L. and S. Streets, but he is out of that now—keeps a first class *Cafe*, and owns a block of houses. Now Paul, here is a splendid chance for you; business is dull, and now accept this opening. Of course I mean to keep a first class saloon. I don't intend to tolerate loafing, or disorderly conduct, or to sell to drunken men. In fact, I shall put up my scale of prices so that you need fear no annoyance from rough, low, boisterous men who don't know how to behave themselves. What say you, Paul?"

"I say, no! I wouldn't engage in such a business, not if it paid me a hundred thousand dollars a year. I think these first class saloons are just as great a curse to the community as the low groggeries, and I look upon them as the fountain heads of the low groggeries. The man who begins to drink in the well lighted and splendidly furnished saloon is in danger of finishing in the lowest dens of vice and shame."

"As you please," said John Anderson stiffly, "I thought that as business is dull that I would show you a chance, that would yield you a handsome profit; but if you refuse, there is no harm done. I know young men who would jump at the chance."

You may think it strange that knowing Paul Clifford as John Anderson did, that he should propose to him an interest in a drinking saloon; but John Anderson was a man who was almost destitute of faith in human goodness. His motto was that "every man has his price," and as business was fairly dull, and Paul was somewhat cramped for want of capital, he thought a good business investment would be the price for Paul Clifford's conscientious scruples.

"Anderson," said Paul looking him calmly in the face, "you may call me visionary and impracticable; but I am determined however poor I may be, never to engage in any business on which I cannot ask God's blessing. And John I am sorry from the bottom of my heart, that you have concluded to give up your grocery and keep a saloon. You cannot keep that saloon without sending a flood of demoralizing influence over the community. Your profit will be the loss of others. Young men will form in that saloon habits which will curse and overshadow all their lives. Husbands and fathers will waste their time and money, and confirm themselves in habits which will bring misery, crime, and degradation; and the fearful outcome of your business will be broken hearted wives, neglected children, outcast men, blighted characters and worse than wasted lives. No not for the wealth of the Indies, would I engage in such a ruinous business, and I am thankful today that I had a dear sainted mother who taught me that it was better to have my hands clear than to have them full. How often would she lay her dear hands upon my head, and clasp my hands in hers and say, 'Paul, I want you to live so that you can always feel that there is no eye before whose glance you will shrink, no voice from whose tones your heart will quail, because your hands are not clean, or your record not pure,' and I feel glad to-day that the precepts and example of that dear mother have given tone and coloring to my life; and though she has been in her grave for many years, her memory and her words are still to me an ever present inspiration."

"Yes Paul; I remember your mother. I wish! Oh well there is no use wishing. But if all Christians were like her, I would have more faith in their religion."

"But John the failure of others is no excuse for our own derelictions."

"Well, I suppose not. It is said, the way Jerusalem was kept clean, every man swept before his own door. And so you will not engage in the business?"

"No John, no money I would earn would be the least inducement."

"How foolish," said John Anderson to himself as they parted. "There is a young man who might succeed splendidly if he would only give up some of his old fashioned notions, and launch out into life as if he had some common sense. If business remains as it is, I think he will find out before long that he has got to shut his eyes and swallow down a great many things he don't like."

After the refusal of Paul Clifford, John soon found a young man of facile conscience who was willing to join with him in a conspiracy of sin against the peace, happiness and welfare of the community. And he spared neither pains nor expense to make his saloon attractive to what he called, "the young bloods of the city," and by these he meant young men whose parents were wealthy, and whose sons had more leisure and spending money than was good for them. He succeeded in fitting up a magnificent palace of sin. Night after night till morning flashed the orient, eager and anxious men sat over the gaming table watching the turn of a card, or the throw of a dice. Sparkling champaign, or ruby-tinted wine were served in beautiful and costly glasses. Rich divans and easy chairs invited weary men to seek repose from unnatural excitement. Occasionally women entered that saloon, but they were women not as God had made them, but as sin had debased them. Women whose costly jewels and magnificent robes were the livery of sin, the outside garnishing of moral death; the flush upon whose cheek, was not the flush of happiness, and the light in their eyes was not the sparkle of innocent joy,—women whose laughter was sadder than their tears, and who were dead while they lived. In that house were wine, and mirth, and revelry, "but the dead were there," men dead to virtue, true honor and rectitude, who walked the streets as other men, laughed, chatted, bought, sold, exchanged and bartered, but whose souls were encased in living tombs, bodies that were dead to righteousness but alive to sin. Like a spider weaving its meshes around the unwary fly, John Anderson wove his network of sin around the young men that entered his saloon. Before they entered there, it was pleasant to see the supple vigor and radiant health that were manifested in the poise of their bodies, the lightness of their eyes, the freshness of their lips and the bloom upon their cheeks. But Oh! it was so sad to see how soon the manly gait would change to the drunkard's stagger. To see eyes once bright with intelligence growing vacant and confused and giving place to the drunkard's leer. In many cases lassitude supplanted vigor, and sickness overmastered health. But the saddest thing was the fearful power that appetite had gained over its victims, and though nature lifted her signals of distress, and sent her warnings through weakened nerves and disturbed functions, and although they were wasting money, time, talents, and health, ruining their characters, and alienating their friends, and bringing untold agony to hearts that loved them and yearned over their defections, yet the fascination grew stronger and ever and anon the grave opened at their feet; and disguise it as loving friends might, the seeds of death had been nourished by the fiery waters of alcohol.

# V

(Text missing.)

## VI

For a few days the most engrossing topic in A.P. was what shall I wear, and what will you wear. There was an amount of shopping to be done, and dressmakers to be consulted and employed before the great event of the season came off. At length the important evening arrived and in the home of Mr. Glossop, a wealthy and retired whiskey dealer, there was a brilliant array of wealth and fashion. Could all the misery his liquor had caused been turned into blood, there would have been enough to have oozed in great drops from every marble ornament or beautiful piece of frescoe that adorned his home, for that home with its beautiful surroundings and costly furniture was the price of blood, but the glamor of his wealth was in the eyes of his guests; and they came to be amused and entertained and not to moralize on his ill-gotten wealth.

The wine flowed out in unstinted measures and some of the women so forgot themselves as to attempt to rival the men in drinking. The barrier being thrown down Charles drank freely, till his tones began to thicken, and his eye to grow muddled, and he sat down near Jeanette and tried to converse; but he was too much under the influence of liquor to hold a sensible and coherent conversation.

"Oh! Charley you naughty boy, that wine has got into your head and you don't know what you are talking about."

"Well, Miss Jenny, I b'lieve you're 'bout half-right, my head does feel funny."

"I shouldn't wonder; mine feels rather dizzy, and Miss Thomas has gone home with a sick headache, and I know what her headaches mean," said Jeanette significantly.

"My head," said Mary Gladstone, "really feels as big as a bucket."

"And I feel real dizzy," said another.

"And so do I," said another, "I feel as if I could hardly stand, I feel awful weak."

"Why girls, you! are all, all, tipsy, now just own right up, and be done with it," said Charles Romaine.

"Why Charlie you are as good as a wizard, I believe we have all got too much wine aboard: but we are not as bad as the girls of B.S., for they succeeded in out drinking the men. I heard the men drank eight bottles of wine, and that they drank sixteen."

Alas for these young people they were sporting upon the verge of a precipice, but its slippery edge was concealed by flowers. They were playing with the firebrands of death and thought they were Roman-candles and harmless rockets.

"Good morning Belle," said Jeanette Roland to her cousin Belle as she entered her cousin's sitting-room the morning after the party and found Jeanette lounging languidly upon the sofa.

"Good morning. It is a lovely day, why are you not out enjoying the fresh air? Can't you put on your things and go shopping with me? I think you have excellent taste and I often want to consult it."

"Well after all then I am of some account in your eyes."

"Of course you are; who said you were not(?)"

"Oh! nobody only I had an idea that you thought that I was as useless as a canary bird."

"I don't think that a canary bird is at all a useless thing. It charms our ears with its song, and pleases our eye with its beauty, and I am a firm believer in the utility of beauty—but can you, or rather will you not go with me?"

"Oh Belle I would, but I am as sleepy as a cat."

"What's the matter?"

"I was up so late last night at Mrs. Glossop's party; but really it was a splendid affair, everything was in the richest profusion, and their house is magnificently furnished. Oh Belle I wish you could have been there."

"I don't; there are two classes of people with whom I never wish to associate, or number as my especial friends, and they are rum sellers and slave holders."

"Oh! well, Mr. Glossop is not in the business now and what is the use of talking about the past; don't be always remembering a man's sins against him."

"Would you say the same of a successful pirate who could fare sumptuously from the effects of his piracy?"

"No I would not; but Belle the cases is not at all parallel."

"Not entirely. One commits his crime against society within the pale of the law, the other commits his outside. They are both criminals against the welfare of humanity. One murders the body, and the other stabs the soul. If I knew that Mr. Glossop was sorry for having been a liquor dealer and was bringing forth fruits meet for repentance, I would be among the first to hail his reformation with heartfelt satisfaction;

but when I hear that while he no longer sells liquor, that he constantly offers it to his guests, I feel that he should rather sit down in sackcloth and ashes than fireside at sumptuous feasts, obtained by liquor selling. When crime is sanctioned by law, and upheld by custom and fashion, it assumes its most dangerous phase; and there is often a fearful fascination in the sin that is environed by success."

"Oh! Belle do stop. I really think that you will go crazy on the subject of temperance. I think you must have written these lines that I have picked up somewhere; let me see what they are,—

*"Tell me not that I hate the bowl,*
*Hate is a feeble word."*

"No Jeanette, I did not write them, but I have felt all the writer has so nervously expressed. In my own sorrow-darkened home, and over my poor father's grave, I learned to hate liquor in any form with all the intensity of my nature."

"Well, it was a good thing you were not at Mrs. Glossop's last night, for some of our heads were rather dizzy, and I know that Mr. Romaine was out of gear. Now Belle! don't look so shocked and pained; I am sorry I told you."

"Yes, I am very sorry. I had great hopes that Mr. Romaine had entirely given up drinking, and I was greatly pained when I saw him take a glass of wine at your solicitation. Jeanette I think Mr. Romaine feels a newly awakened interest in you, and I know that you possess great influence over him. I saw it that night when he hesitated, when you first asked him to drink, and I was so sorry to see that influence. Oh Jeanette instead of being his temptress, try and be the angel that keeps his steps. If Mr. Romaine ever becomes a drunkard and goes down to a drunkard's grave, I cannot help feeling that a large measure of the guilt will cling to your shirts."

"Oh Belle, do stop, or you will give me the horrors. Pa takes wine every day at his dinner and I don't see that he is any worse off for it. If Charles Romaine can't govern himself, I can't see how I am to blame for it."

"I think you are to blame for this Jeanette: (and pardon me if I speak plainly). When Charles Romaine was trying to abstain, you tempted him to break his resolution, and he drank to please you. I wouldn't have done so for my right hand."

"They say old coals are easily kindled, and I shall be somewhat chary about receiving attention from him, if you feel so deeply upon the subject."

"Jeanette you entirely misapprehend me. Because I have ceased to regard Mr. Romaine as a lover, does not hinder me from feeling for him as a friend. And because I am his friend and yours also, I take the liberty to remonstrate against your offering him wine at your entertainments."

"Well Belle, I can't see the harm in it, I don't believe there was another soul who refused except you and Mr. Freeman, and you are so straightlaced, and he is rather green, just fresh from the country, it won't take him long to get citified."

"Citified or countrified, I couldn't help admiring his strength of principle which stood firm in the midst of temptation and would not yield to the blandishments of the hour. And so you will not go out with me this morning?"

"Oh! No Belle, I am too tired. Won't you excuse me?"

"Certainly, but I must go. Good morning."

"What a strange creature my cousin Belle is," said Jeanette, to herself as Miss Gordon left the room. "She will never be like any one else. I don't think she will ever get over my offering Mr. Romaine that glass of wine, I wish she hadn't seen it, but I'll try and forget her and go to sleep."

But Jeanette was not destined to have the whole morning for an unbroken sleep. Soon after Bell's departure the bell rang and Charles Romaine was announced, and weary as Jeanette was, she was too much interested in his society to refuse him; and arraying herself in a very tasteful and becoming manner, she went down to receive him in the parlor.

# VII

Very pleasant was the reception Jeanette Roland gave Mr. Romaine. There was no reproof upon her lips nor implied censure in her manner. True he had been disguised by liquor or to use a softer phrase, had taken too much wine. But others had done the same and treated it as a merry escapade, and why should she be so particular? Belle Gordon would have acted very differently but then she was not Belle, and in this instance she did not wish to imitate her. Belle was so odd, and had become very unpopular, and besides she wished to be very very pleasant to Mr. Romaine. He was handsome, agreeable and wealthy, and she found it more congenial to her taste to clasp hands with him and float down stream together, than help him breast the current of his wrong tendencies, and stand firmly on the rock of principle.

"You are looking very sweet, but rather pensive this morning," said Mr. Romaine, noticing a shadow on the bright and beautiful face of Jeanette, whose color had deepened by the plain remarks of her cousin Belle. "What is the matter?"

"Oh nothing much, only my cousin Belle has been here this morning, and she has been putting me on the stool of repentance."

"Why! what have you been doing that was naughty?"

"Oh! she was perfectly horror-stricken when I told her about the wine we drank and Mrs. Glossop's party. I wish I had not said a word to her about it."

"What did she say?"

"Oh she thought it was awful, the way we were going on. She made me feel that I died (*sic*) something dreadful when I offered you a glass of wine at Ma's silver wedding. I don't believe Belle ever sees a glass of wine, without thinking of murder, suicide and a drunkard's grave."

"But we are not afraid of those dreadful things, are we Jeanette?"

"Of course not, but somehow Belle always makes me feel uncomfortable, when she begins to talk on temperance. She says she is terribly in earnest, and I think she is."

"Miss Gordon and I were great friends once," said Charles Romaine, as a shadow flitted over his face, and a slight sigh escaped his lips.

"Were you? Why didn't you remain so?"

"Because she was too good for me."

"That is a very sorry reason."

"But it is true. I think Miss Gordon is an excellent young lady, but she and I wouldn't agree on the temperance question. The man who marries her has got to toe the mark. She ought to be a minister's wife."

"I expect she will be an old maid."

"I don't know, but if I were to marry her, I should prepare myself to go to Church every Sunday morning and to stay home in the afternoon and repeat my catechism."

"I would like to see you under her discipline."

"It would come hard on a fellow, but I might go farther and fare worse."

"And so you and Belle were great friends, once?"

"Yes, but as we could not agree on the total abstinence question, we parted company."

"How so? Did you part as lovers part?"

> *She with a wronged and broken heart?*
> *And you, rejoicing you were free,*
> *Glad to regain you liberty?*

"Not at all. She gave me the mitten and I had to take it."

"Were you very sorry?"

"Yes, till I met you."

"Oh! Mr. Romaine," said Jeanette blushing and dropping her eyes.

"Why not? I think I have found in your society an ample compensation for the loss of Miss Gordon."

"But I think Belle is better than I am. I sometimes wish I was half so good."

"You are good enough for me; Belle is very good, but somehow her goodness makes a fellow uncomfortable. She is what I call distressingly good; one doesn't want to be treated like a wild beast in a menagerie, and to be every now and then stirred up with a long stick."

"What a comparison!"

"Well it is a fact; when a fellow's been busy all day pouring over Coke and Blackstone, or casting up wearisome rows of figures, and seeks a young lady's society in the evening, he wants to enjoy himself, to bathe in the sunshine of her smiles, and not to be lectured about his shortcomings. I tell you, Jeanette, it comes hard on a fellow."

"You want some one to smooth the wrinkles out of the brow of care, and not to add fresh ones."

"Yes, and I hope it will be my fortune to have a fair soft hand like his," said Mr. Romaine, slightly pressing Jeanette's hand to perform the welcome and agreeable task.

"Belle's hand would be firmer than mine for the talk."

"It is not the strong hand, but the tender hand I want in a woman."

"But Belle is very kind; she did it all for your own good."

"Of course she did; my father used to say so when I was a boy, and he corrected me; but it didn't make me enjoy the correction."

"It is said our best friends are those who show us our faults, and teach us how to correct them."

"My best friend is a dear, sweet girl who sits by my side, who always welcomes me with a smile, and beguiles me so with her conversation, that I take no note of the hours until the striking of the clock warns me it is time to leave; and I should ask no higher happiness than to be permitted to pass all the remaining hours of my life at her side. Can I dare to hope for such a happy fortune?"

A bright flush overspread the cheek of Jeanette Roland; there was a sparkle of joy in her eyes as she seemed intently examining the flowers on her mother's carpet, and she gently referred him to Papa for an answer. In due time Mr. Roland was interviewed, his consent obtained, and Jeanette Roland and Charles Romaine were affianced lovers.

"Girls, have you heard the news?" said Miss Tabitha Jones, a pleasant and wealthy spinster, to a number of young girls who were seated at her tea table.

"No! what is it?"

"I hear Mr. Romaine is to be married next spring."

"To whom?"

"Jeanette Roland."

"Well! I do declare; I thought he was engaged to Belle Gordon."

"I thought so too, but it is said that she refused him, but I don't believe it; I don't believe that she had a chance."

"Well I do."

"Why did she refuse him?"

"Because he would occasionally take too much wine."

"But he is not a drunkard."

"But she dreads that he will be."

"Well! I think it is perfectly ridiculous. I gave Belle credit for more common sense. I think he was one of the most eligible gentlemen in our set. Wealthy, handsome and agreeable. What could have possessed Belle? I think he is perfectly splendid."

"Yes said another girl, I think Belle stood very much in her own light. She is not rich, and if she would marry him she could have everything heart could wish. What a silly girl! You wouldn't catch me throwing away such a chance."

"I think," said Miss Tabitha, "that instead of Miss Gordon's being a silly girl, that she has acted both sensibly and honorably in refusing to marry a man she could not love. No woman should give her hand where she cannot yield her heart."

"But Miss Tabitha, the strangest thing to me is, that I really believe that Belle Gordon cares more for Mr. Romaine than she does for any one else; her face was a perfect study that night at Mrs. Roland's party."

"How so?"

"They say that after Miss Gordon requested Mr. Romaine, that for a while he scrupulously abstained from taking even a glass of wine. At several entertainments, he adhered to this purpose but on the evening of Mrs. Roland's silver wedding Jeanette succeeded in persuading him to take a glass, in honor of the occasion. I watched Belle's face and it was a perfect study, every nerve seemed quivering with intense anxiety. Once I think she reached out her hand unconsciously as if to snatch away the glass, and when at last he yielded I saw the light fade from her eyes, a deadly pallor overspread her cheek, and I thought at one time she was about to faint, but she did not, and only laid her head upon her side as if to allay a sudden spasm of agony."

# VIII

Paul Clifford sat at his ledger with a perplexed and anxious look. It was near two o'clock and his note was in bank. If he could not raise five hundred dollars by three o'clock, that note would be protested. Money was exceedingly hard to raise, and he was about despairing. Once he thought of applying to John Anderson, but he said to himself, "No, I will not touch his money, for it is the price of blood," for he did not wish to owe gratitude where he did not feel respect. It was now five minutes past two o'clock and in less than an hour his note would be protested unless relief came from some unexpected quarter.

"Is Mr. Clifford in?" said a full manly voice. Paul, suddenly roused from his painful reflections, answered, "Yes, come in. Good morning sir, what can I do for you this morning?"

"I have come to see you on business."

"I am at your service," said Paul.

"Do you remember," said the young man, "of having aided an unfortunate friend more than a dozen years since by lending him five hundred dollars?"

"Yes, I remember he was an old friend of mine, a school-mate of my father's, Charles Smith."

"Well I am his son, and I have come to liquidate my father's debt. Here is the money with interest for twelve years."

Paul's heart gave a sudden bound of joy. Strong man as he was a mist gathered in his eyes as he reached out his hand to receive the thrice welcome sum. He looked at the clock, it was just fifteen minutes to three.

"Will you walk with me to the bank or wait till I return?"

"I will wait," said James Smith, taking up the morning paper.

"You are just in time, Mr. Clifford," said the banker smiling and bowing as Paul entered, "I was afraid your note would be protested; but it is all right."

"Yes," said Paul, "the money market is very tight, but I think I shall weather the storm."

"I hope so, you may have to struggle hard for awhile to keep your head above the water; but you must take it for your motto that there is no such word as 'fail.'"

"Thank you, good morning."

"Well Mr. Smith," said Paul when he returned, "your father and mine were boys together. He was several years younger than my father, and a great favorite in our family among the young folks. About twelve years since when I had just commenced business, I lent him five hundred dollars, and when his business troubles became complicated I refused to foreclose a mortgage which I had on his home. An acquaintance of mine sneered at my lack of business keenness, and predicted that my money would be totally lost, when I told him perhaps it was the best investment I ever made." He smiled incredulously and said, "I would rather see it than hear of it: but I will say that in all my business career I never received any money that came so opportune as this. It reminds me of the stories that I have read in fairy books. People so often fail in paying their own debts, it seems almost a mystery to me that you should pay a debt contracted by your father when you were but a boy."

"The clue to this mystery has been the blessed influence of my sainted mother;" and a flush of satisfaction mantled his cheek as he referred to her.

"After my father's death my mother was very poor. When she looked into the drawer there were only sixty cents in money. Of course, he had some personal property, but it was not immediately available like money, but through the help of kind friends she was enabled to give him a respectable funeral. Like many other women in her condition of life, she had been brought up in entire ignorance of managing any other business, than that which belonged to her household. For years she had been shielded in the warm clasp of loving arms, but now she had to bare her breast to the storm and be father and mother both to her little ones. My father as you know died in debt, and he was hardly in his grave when his creditors were upon her track. I have often heard her speak in the most grateful manner of your forbearance and kindness to her in her hour of trouble. My mother went to see my father's principal creditor and asked him only to give her a little time to straighten out the tangled threads of her business, but he was inexorable, and said that he had waited and lost by it. Very soon he had an administrator appointed by the court, who in about two months took the business in his hands; and my mother was left to struggle along with her little ones, and face an uncertain future. These were dark days but we managed to live through them. I have often heard her say that she lived by faith and not sight, that poverty had its compensations, that there was something very sweet in a life of simple trust, to her, God was not some far off and unapproachable force in the universe, the unconscious Creator of all consciousness, the unperceiving author of all perception, but a Friend and a Father coming near to her in sorrows, taking cognizance of her grief, and gently smoothing her path in life. But it was not only by precept that she taught us; her life was a living epistle. One morning as the winter was advancing I heard her say she hoped she would be able to get a nice woolen shawl, as hers was getting worse for wear. Shortly after I went out into the street and found a roll of money lying at my feet. Oh I remember it as well as if it had just occurred. How my heart bounded with joy. 'Here,' I said to myself, 'is money enough to buy mother a shawl and bonnet. Oh I am so glad,' and hurrying home I laid it in her lap and said with boyish glee, 'Hurrah for your new shawl; look what I found in the street.'"

"What is it my son?" she said.

"Why here is money enough to buy you a new shawl and bonnet too." It seems as if I see her now, as she looked, when she laid it aside, and said—

"But James, it is not ours?"

"Not ours, mother, why I found it in the street!"

"Still it is not ours."

"Why mother ain't you going to keep it?"

"No my son, I shall go down to the *Clarion* office and advertise it."

"But mother why not wait till it is advertised?"

"And what then?"

"If there is no owner for it, then we can keep it."

"James" she said calmly and sadly, "I am very sorry to see you so ready to use what is not your own. I should not feel that I was dealing justly, if I kept this money without endeavoring to find the owner."

"I confess that I was rather chopfallen at her decision, but in a few days after advertising we found the rightful owner. She was a very poor woman who had saved by dint of hard labor the sum of twenty dollars, and was on her way to pay the doctor who had attended her during a spell of rheumatic fever, when she lost the money and had not one dollar left to pay for advertising and being disheartened, she had given up all hope of finding it, when she happened to see it advertised in the paper. She was very grateful to my mother for restoring the money and offered her some compensation, but she refused to take it, saying she had only done her duty, and would have been ashamed of herself had she not done so. Her conduct on this occasion made an impression on my mind that has never been erased. When I grew older she explained to me about my father's affairs, and uncancelled debts, and I resolved that I would liquidate every just claim against him, and take from his memory even the shadow of a reproach. To this end I have labored late and early; to-day I have paid the last claim against him, and I am a free man."

"But how came you to find me and pay me to-day?" "I was purchasing in Jones & Brother's store, when you came in to borrow money, and I heard Jones tell his younger brother that he was so sorry that he could not help you, and feared that you would be ruined."

"Who is he?" said I, "for out West I had lost track of you."

"He is Paul Clifford, a friend of your father's. Can you help him? He is perfectly reliable. We would trust him with ten thousand dollars if we had it. Can you do anything for him? we will go his security, he is a fine fellow and we hate to see him go under."

"Yes" said I, "he was one of my father's creditors and I have often heard my mother speak of his generosity to her little ones, and I am glad that I have the privilege of helping him. I immediately went to the bank had a note cashed and I am very glad if I have been of any special service to you."

"You certainly have been, and I feel that a heavy load had been lifted from my heart."

Years ago Paul Clifford sowed the seeds of kindness and they were yielding him a harvest of satisfaction.

# IX

## Belle Gordon

B elle Gordon was a Christian; she had learned or tried to realize what is meant by the apostle Paul when he said, "Ye are bought with a price." To her those words meant the obligation she was under to her heavenly Father, for the goodness and mercy that had surrounded her life, for the patience that had borne with her errors and sins, and above all for the gift of his dear Son, the ever blessed Christ. Faith to her was not a rich traditional inheritance, a set of formulated opinions, received without investigation, and adopted without reflection. She could not believe because others did, and however plausible or popular a thing might be she was too conscientious to say she believed it if she did not, and when she became serious on the subject of religion it was like entering into a wilderness of doubt and distress. She had been taught to look upon God, more as the great and dreadful God, than as the tender loving Father of his human children, and so strong was the power of association, that she found it hard to believe that God is good, and yet until she could believe this there seemed to be no resting place for her soul; but in course of time the shadows were lifted from her life. Faith took the place of doubting, and in the precious promises of the Bible she felt that her soul had found a safe and sure anchorage. If others believed because they had never doubted, she believed because she had doubted and her doubts had been dispelled by the rays of heaven, and believing, she had entered into rest. Feeling that she was bought with a price, she realized that she was not her own, but the captive of Divine Love, and that her talents were not given her to hide beneath a bushel or to use for merely selfish enjoyments. That her time was not her own to be frittered away by the demands of fashion or to be spent in unavailing regrets. Every reform which had for its object the lessening of human misery, or the increase of human happiness, found in her an earnest ally. On the subject of temperance she was terribly in earnest. Every fiber of her heart responded to its onward movement. There was no hut or den where human beings congregated that she felt was too vile or too repulsive to enter, if by so doing she could help lift some fallen soul out of the depths of sin and degradation. While some doubted the soundness of her religious opinions, none doubted the orthodoxy of her life. Little children in darkened homes smiled as the sunlight of her presence came over their paths; reformed men looked upon her as a loving counsellor and faithful friend and sister; women wretched and sorrowful, dragged down from love and light, by the intemperance of their husbands, brought to her their heavy burdens, and by her sympathy and tender consideration she helped them bear them. She was not rich in this world's goods, but she was affluent in tenderness, sympathy, and love, and out of the fullness of her heart, she was a real minister of mercy among the poor and degraded. Believing that the inner life developed the outer, she considered the poor, and strove to awaken within them self-reliance, and self-control, feeling that one of the surest ways to render people helpless or dangerous is to crush out their self-respect and self-reliance. She thought it one of the greatest privileges of her life to be permitted to scatter flowers by the wayside of life. Other women might write beautiful poems; she did more. She made her life a thing of brightness and beauty.

"Do you think she will die?" said Belle Gordon, bending tenderly over a pale and fainting woman, whose face in spite of its attenuation showed traces of great beauty.

"Not if she is properly cared for; she has fainted from exhaustion brought on by overwork and want of proper food." Tears gathered in the eyes of Belle Gordon as she lifted the beautiful head upon her lap and chafed the pale hands to bring back warmth and circulation.

"Let her be removed to her home as soon as possible," said the doctor. "The air is too heavy and damp for her."

"I wonder where she lives," said Belle thoughtfully, scanning her face, as the features began to show returning animation.

"Round the corner," said an urchin, "she's Joe Cough's wife. I seed her going down the street with a great big bundle, and Mam said, she looked like she was going to topple over."

"Where is her husband?"

"I don't know, I 'spec he's down to Jim Green's saloon."

"What does he do?"

"He don't do nothing, but Mam says she works awful hard. Come this way," said he with a quickness gathered by his constant contact with street life.

Up two flights of rickety stairs they carried the wasted form of Mary Gough, and laid her tenderly upon a clean but very poor bed. In spite of her extreme poverty there was an air of neatness in the desolate room. Belle looked around and found an old tea pot in which there were a few leaves. There were some dry crusts in the cupboard, while two little children crouched by the embers in the grate, and cried for the mother. Belle soon found a few coals in an old basin with which she replenished the fire, and covering up the sick woman as carefully as she could, stepped into the nearest grocery and replenished her basket with some of good the things of life.

"Is it not too heavy for you(r) might?" said Paul Clifford from whose grocery Belle had bought her supplies.

"Can I not send them home for you?"

"No I don't want them sent home. They are for a poor woman and her suffering children, who live about a square from here in Lear's Court." Paul stood thoughtfully a moment before handing her the basket, and said—"That court has a very bad reputation; had I not better accompany you? I hope you will not consider my offer as an intrusion, but I do not think it is safe for you to venture there alone."

"If you think it is not safe I will accept of your company; but I never thought of danger for myself in the presence of that fainting woman and her hungry children. Do you know her? Her name is Mrs. Gough."

"I think I do. If it is the person I mean, I remember her when she was as lighthearted and happy a girl as I ever saw, but she married against her parents' consent, a worthless fellow named Joe Gough, and in a short time she disappeared from the village and I suppose she has come home, broken in health and broken in spirit."

"And I am afraid she has come home to die. Are her parents still alive?"

"Yes, but her father never forgave her. Her mother I believe would take her to her heart as readily as she ever did, but her husband has an iron will and she has got to submit to him."

"Where do they live?"

"At No 200 Rouen St. but here we are at the door." Paul carried the basket up stairs, and sat down quietly, while Belle prepared some refreshing tea and toast for the feeble mother; and some bread and milk for the hungry children.

"What shall I do?" said Belle looking tenderly upon the wan face, "I hate to leave her alone and yet I confess I do not prefer spending the night here."

"Of course not," said Paul looking thoughtfully into the flickering fire of the grate.

"Oh! I have it now; I know a very respectable woman who occasionally cleans out my store. Just wait a few moments, and I think I can find her," said Paul Clifford turning to the door. In a short time he returned bringing with him a pleasant looking woman whose face in spite of the poverty of her dress had a look of genuine refinement which comes not so much from mingling with people of culture as from the culture of her own moral and spiritual nature. She had learned to "look up and not to look down." To lend a helping hand wherever she felt it was needed. Her life was spent in humble usefulness. She was poor in this world's goods, but rich in faith and good works. No poor person who asked her for bread ever went away empty. Sometimes people would say, "I wouldn't give him a mouthful; he is not worthy," and then she would say in the tenderest and sweetest manner:

"Suppose our heavenly Father only gave to us because we are worthy; what would any of us have?" I know she once said of a miserable sot with whom she shared her scanty food, that he is a wretched creature, but I wanted to get at his heart, and the best way to it was through his stomach. I never like to preach religion to hungry people. There is something very beautiful about the charity of the poor, they give not as the rich of their abundance, but of their limited earnings, gifts which when given in a right spirit bring a blessing with them.

# X

## Mary Gough

I think," said Paul Clifford to Miss Gordon, "that I have found just the person that will suit you, and if you accept I will be pleased to see you safe home." Belle thanked the young grocer, and gratefully accepted his company.

Belle returned the next day to see her protege and found her getting along comfortably although she could not help seeing it was sorrow more than disease that was sapping her life, and drying up the feeble streams of existence.

"How do you feel this morning?" said Belle laying her hand tenderly upon her forehead.

"Better, much better," she replied with an attempt at cheerfulness in her voice. "I am so glad, that Mother Graham is here. It is like letting the sunshine into these gloomy rooms to have her around. It all seems like a dream to me, I remember carrying a large bundle of work to the store, that my employer spoke harshly to me and talked of cutting down my wages. I also remember turning into the street, my eyes almost blinded with tears, and that I felt a dizziness in my head. The next I remember was seeing a lady feeding my children, and a gentleman coming in with Aunty Graham."

"Yes," said Belle, "fortunately after I had seen you, I met with Mr. Clifford who rendered me every necessary assistance. His presence was very opportune," just then Belle turned her eyes toward the door and saw Mr. Clifford standing on the threshold.

"Ah," said he smiling and advancing "this time the old adage has failed, which says that listeners never hear any good of themselves; for without intending to act the part of an eavesdropper, I heard myself pleasantly complimented."

"No more than you deserve," said Belle smiling and blushing, as she gave him her hand in a very frank and pleasant manner. "Mrs. Gough is much better this morning and is very grateful to you for your kindness."

"Mine," said Mr. Clifford "if you, will call it so, was only the result of an accident. Still I am very glad if I have been of any service, and you are perfectly welcome to make demands upon me that will add to Mrs. Cough's comfort."

"Thank you, I am very glad she has found a friend in you. It is such a blessed privilege to be able to help others less fortunate than ourselves."

"It certainly is."

"Just a moment," said Belle, as the voice of Mrs. Gough fell faintly on her ear.

"What is it, dear?" said Belle bending down to catch her words. "Who is that gentleman? His face and voice seem familiar."

"It is Mr. Clifford."

"Paul Clifford?"

"Yes. Do you know him?"

"Yes, I knew him years ago when I was young and happy; but it seems an age since. Oh, isn't it a dreadful thing, to be a drunkard's wife?"

"Yes it is, but would you like to speak to Mr. Clifford?"

"Yes! Mam, I would."

"Mr. Clifford," said Belle, "Mrs. Gough would like to speak with you."

"Do you not know me?" said Mary, looking anxiously into his face.

"I recognized you as soon as you moved into the neighborhood."

"I am very glad. I feared that I was so changed that my own dear mother would hardly recognize me. Don't you think she would pity and forgive me, if she saw what a mournful wretch I am?"

"Yes, I think she has long forgiven you and longs to take you to her heart as warmly as she ever did."

"And my father?"

"I believe he would receive you, but I don't think he would be willing to recognize your husband. You know he is very set in his ways."

"Mr. Clifford, I feel that my days are numbered and that my span of life will soon be done; but while I live I feel it my duty to cling to my demented husband, and to do all I can to turn him from the error of his ways. But I do so wish that my poor children could have my mother's care, when I am gone. If I were satisfied on that score, I would die content."

"Do not talk of dying," said Belle taking the pale thin hand in hers. "You must try and live for your children's sake. When you get strong I think I can find you some work among my friends. There is Mrs. Roberts, she often gives out work and I think I will apply to her."

"Mrs. James Roberts on St. James St. near 16th?"

"Yes! do you know her?"

"Yes," said Mrs. Gough closing her eyes wearily, "I know her and have worked for her."

"I think she is an excellent woman, I remember one morning we were talking together on religious experience, and about women speaking in class and conference meetings. I said I did not think I should like to constantly relate my experience in public, there was often such a lack of assurance of faith about me that I shrank from holding up my inner life to inspection; and she replied that she would always say that she loved Jesus, and I thought Oh, how I would like to have her experience. What rest and peace I would have if I could feel that I was always in harmony with Him."

"Miss Belle I hope you will not be offended with me, for I am very ignorant about these matters; but there was something about Mrs. Roberts dealings with us poor working people, that did seem to me not to be just what I think religion calls for. I found her a very hard person to deal with; she wanted so much work for so little money."

"But, Mrs. Gough, the times are very hard; and the rich feel it as well as the poor."

"But not so much. It curtails them in their luxuries, and us in our necessities; perhaps I shouldn't mention, but after my husband had become a confirmed drunkard, and all hope had died out of my heart, I hadn't time to sit down and brood helplessly over my misery. I had to struggle for my children and if possible keep the wolf from the door; and besides food and clothing, I wanted to keep my children in a respectable neighborhood, and my whole soul rose up in revolt against the idea of bringing them up where their eyes and ears would be constantly smitten by improper sights and sounds. While I was worrying over my situation and feeling that my health was failing under the terrible pressure of care and overwork, Mrs. Roberts brought me work; 'What will you do this for,' she said, displaying one of the articles she wanted made. I replied, 'One dollar and twenty-five cents,' and I knew the work well worth it. 'I can get it done for one dollar,' she replied, 'and I am not willing to give any more.' What could I do? I was out of work, my health was poor, and my children clutching at my heart strings for bread; and so I took it at her price. It was very unprofitable, but it was better than nothing."

"Why that is very strange. I know she pays her dressmaker handsomely."

"That is because her dressmaker is in a situation to dictate her own terms; but while she would pay her a large sum for dressmaking, she would screw and pinch a five-cent piece from one who hadn't power to resist her demands. I have seen people save twenty-five or fifty cents in dealing with poor people, who would squander ten times as much on some luxury of the table or wardrobe. I often find that meanness and extravagance go hand in hand."

"Yes, that is true, still Mrs. Gough, I think people often act like Mrs. Roberts more from want of thought than want of heart. It was an old charge brought against the Israelite, 'My people doth not consider.'"

"WHAT IS THE MATTER, MY dear?" said Belle a few mornings after this conversation as she approached the bedside of Mary Gough, "I thought you were getting along so nicely, and that with proper care you would be on your feet in a few days, but this morning you look so feeble, and seem so nervous and depressed. Do tell me what has happened and what has become of your beautiful hair; oh you had such a wealth of tresses, I really loved to toy with them. Was your head so painful that the doctor ordered them to be cut?"

"Oh, no," she said burying her face in the pillow and breaking into a paroxysm of tears. "Oh, Miss Belle, how can I tell you," she replied recovering from her sudden outburst of sorrow.

"Why, what is it darling? I am at a loss to know what has become of your beautiful hair."

With gentle womanly tact Belle saw that the loss of her hair was a subject replete with bitter anguish, and turning to the children she took them in her lap and interested and amused them by telling beautiful fairy stories. In a short time Mary's composure returned, and she said, "Miss Belle, I can now tell you how I lost my hair. Last night my husband, or the wreck of what was once my husband, came home. His eyes were wild and bloodshot; his face was pale and haggard, his gait uneven, and his hand trembling. I have seen him suffering from *Manipaotu* and dreaded lest he should have a returning of it. Mrs. Graham had just stepped out, and there was no one here but myself and children. He held in his hand a pair of shears, and approached my bedside. I was ready to faint with terror, when he exclaimed, 'Mary I must have liquor or I shall go wild,' he caught my hair in his hand; I was too feeble to resist, and in a few minutes he had cut every lock from my head, and left it just as you see it."

"Oh, what a pity, and what a shame."

"Oh, Miss Gordon do you think the men who make our laws ever stop to consider the misery, crime and destruction that flow out of the liquor traffic? I have done all I could to induce him to abstain, and he has abstained several months at a time and then suddenly like a flash of lightning the temptation returns and all his resolutions are scattered like chaff before the wind. I have been blamed for living with him, but Miss Belle were you to see him in his moments of remorse, and hear his bitter self reproach, and his earnest resolutions to reform, you would as soon leave a drowning man to struggle alone in the water as to forsake him in his weakness when every one else has turned against him, and if I can be the means of saving him, the joy for his redemption will counterbalance all that I have suffered as a drunkard's wife."

# XI

(Text missing.)

# XII

(Text missing.)

# XIII

## John Anderson's Saloon

*"The end of these things is death."*

W hy do you mix that liquor with such care and give it to that child? You know he is not going to pay you for it?"

"I am making an investment."

"How so?"

"Why you see that boy's parents are very rich, and in course of time he will be one of my customers."

"Well! John Anderson as old a sinner as I am, I wouldn't do such a thing for my right hand."

"What's the harm? You are one of my best customers, did liquor ever harm you?"

"Yes it does harm me, and when I see young men beginning to drink, I feel like crying out, 'Young man you are in danger, don't put your feet in the terrible flood, for ten to one you will be swamped.'"

"Well! this is the best joke of the season: Tom Cary preaching temperance. When do you expect to join the Crusade? But, Oh! talk is cheap."

"Cheap or dear, John Anderson, when I saw you giving liquor to that innocent boy, I couldn't help thinking of my poor Charley. He was just such a bright child as that, with beautiful brown eyes, and a fine forehead. Ah that boy had a mind; he was always ahead in his studies. But once when he was about twelve years old, I let him go on a travelling tour with his uncle. He was so agreeable and wide awake, his uncle liked to have him for company; but it was a dear trip to my poor Charley. During this journey they stopped at a hotel, and my brother gave him a glass of wine. Better for my dear boy had he given him a glass of strychnine. That one glass awakened within him a dreadful craving. It raged like a hungry fire. I talked to him, his mother pled with him, but it was no use, liquor was his master, and when he couldn't get liquor I've known him to break into his pantry to get our burning fluid to assuage his thirst. Sometimes he would be sober for several weeks at a time, and then our hopes would brighten that Charley would

FRANCES ELLEN WATKINS HARPER

be himself again, and then in an hour all our hopes would be dashed to the ground. It seemed as if a spell was upon him. He married a dear good girl, who was as true as steel, but all her entreaties for him to give up drinking were like beating the air. He drank, and drank, until he drank himself into the grave."

By this time two or three loungers had gathered around John Anderson and Thomas Gary, and one of them said, "Mr. Gary you have had sad experience, why don't you give up drinking yourself?"

"Give it up! because I can't. To-day I would give one half of my farm if I could pass by this saloon and not feel that I wanted to come in. No, I feel that I am a slave. There was a time when I could have broken my chain, but it is too late now, and I say young men take warning by me and don't make slaves and fools of yourselves."

"Now, Tom Cary," said John Anderson, "it is time for you to dry up, we have had enough of this foolishness, if you can't govern yourself, the more's the pity for you."

Just then the newsboy came along crying: *"Evening Mail. All about the dreadful murder! John Coots and James Loraine. Last edition. Buy a paper, Sir! Here's your last edition, all 'bout the dreadful murder".*

"John Coots," said several voices all at once, "Why he's been here a half dozen times today."

"I've drank with him," said one, "at that bar twice since noon. He had a strange look out of his eyes; and I heard him mutter something to himself."

"Yes," said another, "I heard him say he was going to kill somebody, 'one or the other's got to die,' what does the paper say?"

"LOVE, JEALOUSY, AND MURDER."

"The old story," said Anderson, looking somewhat relieved, "A woman's at the bottom of it."

"And liquor," said Tom Cary, "is at the top of it."

"I wish you would keep a civil tongue in your head," said Anderson, scowling at Cary.

"Oh! never mind; Tom, will have his say. He's got a knack of speaking out in meeting."

"And a very disagreeable knack it is."

"Oh never mind about Tom, read about the murder, and tend to Tom some other time."

Eagerly and excitedly they read the dreadful news. A woman, frail and vicious, was at the bottom; a woman that neither of those men would have married as a gracious gift, was the guilty cause of one murder, and when the law would take its course, two deaths would lie at her door. Oh, the folly of some men, who, instead of striving to make home a thing of beauty, strength and grace, wander into forbidden pastures, and reap for themselves harvests of misery and disgrace. And all for what? Because of the allurements of some idle, vain and sinful woman who has armed herself against the peace, the purity and the progress of the fireside. Such women are the dry rot in the social fabric; they dig in the dark beneath the foundation stones of the home. Young men enter their houses, and over the mirror of their lives, comes the shadow of pollution. Companionship with them unprepares them for the pure, simple joys of a happy and virtuous home; a place which should be the best school for the affections; one of the fairest spots on earth and one of the brightest types of heaven. Such a home as this, may exist without wealth, luxury or display; but it cannot exist without the essential elements of purity, love and truth.

The story was read, and then came the various comments.

"Oh, it was dreadful," said one. "Mr. Loraine belongs to one of the first families in the town; and what a cut it will be to them, not simply that he has been murdered, but murdered where he was—in the house of Lizzie Wilson. I knew her before she left husband and took to evil courses."

"Oh, what a pity, I expect it will almost kill his wife, poor thing, I pity her from the bottom of my heart."

"Why what's the matter Harry Richards? You look as white as a sheet, and you are all of a tremor."

"I've just come from the coroner's inquest, had to be one of the witnesses. I am afraid it will go hard with Coots."

"Why? What was the verdict of the jury?"

"They brought in a verdict of death by killing at the hands of John Coots."

"Were you present at the murder?"

"Yes."

"How did it happen?"

"Why you see John had been spending his money very freely on Lizzie Wilson, and he took it into his head because Loraine had made her some costly presents, that she had treated him rather coolly and wanted to ship him, and so he got dreadfully put out with Loraine and made some bitter threats against him. But I don't believe he would have done the deed if he had been sober, but he's been on a spree for several days and he was half crazy when he did it. Oh it was heartrending to see Loraine's wife when they brought him home a corpse. She gave an awful shriek and fell to the floor, stiff as a poker; and his poor little children, it made my heart bleed to look at them; and his poor old mother. I am afraid it will be the death of her."

In a large city with its varied interests, one event rapidly chases the other. Life-boats are stranded on the shores of time, pitiful wrecks of humanity are dashed amid the rocks and reefs of existence. Old faces disappear and new ones take their places and the stream of life ever hurries on to empty where death's waters meet.

At the next sitting of the Court John Coots was arraigned, tried, and convicted of murder in the first degree. His lawyer tried to bring in a plea of emotional insanity but failed. If insane he was insane through the influence of strong drink. It was proven that he had made fierce threats against the life of Loraine, and the liquor in which he had so freely indulged had served to fire his brain and nerve his hand to carry out his wicked intent; and so the jury brought in its verdict, and he was sentenced to be executed, which sentence was duly performed and that closed another act of the sad drama. Intemperance and Sensuality had clasped hands together, and beneath their cruel fostering the gallows had borne its dreadful fruit of death. The light of one home had been quenched in gloom and guilt. A husband had broken over the barriers that God placed around the path of marital love, and his sun had gone down at mid-day. The sun which should have gilded the horizon of life and lent it additional charms, had gone down in darkness, yes, set behind the shadow of a thousand clouds. Innocent and unoffending childhood was robbed of a father's care, and a once happy wife, and joyful mother sat down in her widow's weeds with the mantle of a gloomier sorrow around her heart. And all for what? Oh who will justify the ways of God to man? Who will impress upon the mind of youth with its impulsiveness that it is a privilege as well as a duty to present the body to God, as a living sacrifice holy and acceptable in his sight. That God gives man no law that is not for his best advantage, and that the interests of humanity, and the laws of purity and self-denial all lie in the same direction, and the man who does not take care of his body must fail to take the best care of his soul; for the body should be temple for God's holy spirit and the instrument to do his work, and we have no right to defile the one or blunt the other and thus render ourselves unfit for the Master's service.

## XIV

B elle Gordon's indignation was thoroughly aroused by hearing Mary Gough's story about the loss of her hair, and she made up her mind that when she saw Joe Gough she would give him a very plain talking.

"I would like to see your husband; I would just like to tell him what I think about his conduct."

"Oh," said Mary, her pale cheek growing whiter with apprehension; "That's his footsteps now, Miss Belle don't say anything to him, Joe's as good and kind a man as I ever saw when he is sober, but sometimes he is really ugly when he has been drinking."

Just then the door was opened, and Joe Gough entered, or rather all that remained of the once witty, talented and handsome Josiah Gough. His face was pale and haggard, and growing premature by age, his wealth of raven hair was unkempt and hung in tangled locks over his forehead, his hand was unsteady and trembling from extreme nervousness, but he was sober enough to comprehend the situation, and to feel a deep sense of remorse and shame, when he gazed upon the weary head from whence he had bereft its magnificent covering.

"Here Mary," said he approaching the bed, "I've brought you a present; I only had four cents, and I thought this would please you, I know you women are so fond of jew-gaws," and he handed (her) a pair of sleeve buttons.

"Thank you," said she, as a faint smile illuminated her pallid cheek. "This," she said turning to Miss Gordon, "is my husband, Josiah Gough."

"Good morning, Mr. Gough," said Belle bowing politely and extending her hand. Joe returned the salutation very courteously and very quietly, sitting down by the bedside, made some remarks about the dampness of the weather. Mary lay very quiet, looking pitifully upon the mour(n)ful wretch at her side, who seemed to regard her and her friend with intense interest. It seemed from his countenance that remorse and shame were rousing up his better nature. Once he rose as if to go—stood irresolutely for a moment, and then sitting down by the bedside, clasped her thin pale hand in his with a caressing motion, and said, "Mary you've had a hard time, but I hope there are better days in store for us, don't get out of heart," and there was a moisture in his eyes in which for a moment beamed a tender, loving light. Belle immediately felt her indignation changing to pity. Surely she thought within herself, this man is worth saving—There is still love and tenderness within him, notwithstanding all his self-ruin, he reminds me of an expression I have picked up somewhere about "Old Oak," holding the young fibres at its heart, I will appeal to that better nature, I will use it as a lever to lift him from the depths into which he has fallen. While she was thinking of the best way to approach him, and how to reach that heart into whose hidden depths she had so unexpectedly glanced, he arose and bending over his wife imprinted upon her lips a kiss in which remorse and shame seemed struggling for expression, and left the room.

"Mother Graham," said Belle, "a happy thought has just struck me, Couldn't we induce Mr. Gough to attend the meeting of the Reform Club? Mr. R.N. speaks tonight and he has been meeting with glorious success as a Temperance Reformer, hundreds of men, many of them confirmed drunkards, have joined, and he is doing a remarkable work, he does not wait for the drunkards to come to him, he goes to them, and wins them by his personal sympathy, and it is wonderful the good he has done, I do wish he would go."

"I wish so too," said Martha Graham.

"If he should not return while I am here will you invite him to attend? Perhaps Mrs. Gough can spare you an hour or two this evening to accompany him."

"That I would gladly do, I think it would do me more good than all the medicines you could give me, to see my poor husband himself once more. Before he took to drinking, I was so happy, but it seems as if since then I have suffered sorrow by the spoonful. Oh the misery that this drink causes. I do hope these reform clubs will be the means of shutting up every saloon in the place, for just as long as one of them is open he is in danger."

"Yes," said Belle, "what we need is not simply to stop the men from drinking, but to keep the temptation out of their way."

"Joe," said Mary, "belongs to a good family, he has a first-rate education, is a fine penman, and a good bookkeeper, but this dreadful drink has thrown him out of some of the best situations in the town where we were living."

"Oh what a pity, I heard Mr. Clifford say that his business was increasing so that he wanted a good clerk and salesman to help him, that he was overworked and crippled for want of sufficient help. Maybe if your husband would sign the pledge, Mr. Clifford would give him a trial, but it is growing late and I must go. I would liked to have seen your husband before I left, and have given him a personal invitation, but you and Mother Graham can invite him for me, so good bye, keep up a good heart, you know where to cast your burden."

Just as Miss Gordon reached the landing, she saw Joe Gough standing at the outer door and laying her hand gently upon his shoulder, exclaimed, "Oh Mr. Gough, I am so glad to see you again, I wanted to invite you to attend a temperance meeting tonight at Amory Hall. Will you go?"

"Well I don't like to promise," he replied, looking down upon his seedy coat and dilapidated shoes.

"Never mind your wardrobe," said Miss Gordon divining his thoughts. "The soul is more than raiment, 'the world has room for another man and I want you to fill the place.'"

"Well," said he, "I'll come."

"Very well, I expect to be there and will look for you. Come early and bring Mother Graham."

"Mrs. Gough can spare her an hour or two this evening, I think your wife is suffering more from exhaustion and debility than anything else."

"Yes poor Mary has had a hard time, but it shan't be always so. As soon as I get work I mean to take her out of this," said he looking disdainfully at the wretched tenement house, with its broken shutters and look of general decay.

"Why Mother Graham is (the) meeting over? You must have had a fine time, you just look delighted. Did Joe go in with you, and where is he now?"

"Yes, he went with me, listened to the speeches, and joined the club, I saw him do it with my own eyes, Oh, we had a glorious time!"

"Oh I am so glad," said Mary, her eyes filling with sudden tears. "I do hope he will keep his pledge!"

"I hope so too, and I hope he will get something to do. Mr. Clifford was there when he signed, and Miss Belle was saying today that he wanted a clerk that would be a first r(at)e place for Joe, if he will only keep his pledge. Mr. Clifford is an active temperance man, and I believe would help to keep Joe straight."

"I hope he'll get the place, but Mother Graham, tell me all about the meeting, you don't know how happy I am."

"Don't I deary? Have I been through it all, but it seems as if I had passed through suffering into peace, but never mind Mother Graham's past troubles, let me tell you about the meeting."

"At these meetings quite a number of people speak, just as we went in one of the speakers was telling his experience, and what a terrible struggle he had to overcome the power of appetite. Now when he felt the fearful craving coming over him he would walk the carpet till he had actually worn it threadbare; but that he had been converted and found grace to help him in time of need, and how he had gone out and tried to reform others and had seen the work prosper in his hand. I watched Joe's face, it seemed lit up with earnestness and hope, as if that man had brought him a message of deliverance; then after the meeting came the signing of the pledge and joining the reform club, and it would have done you good to see the men that joined."

"Do you remember Thomas Allison?"

"Yes, poor fellow, and I think if any man ever inherited drunkenness, he did, for his father and his mother were drunkards before him."

"Well, he joined and they have made him president of the club."

"Well did I ever! But tell me all about Joe."

"When the speaking was over, Joe sat still and thoughtful as if making up his mind, when Miss Gordon came to him and asked him to join, he stopped a minute to button his coat and went right straight up and had his name put down, but oh how the people did clap and shout. Well as Joe was one of the last to sign, the red ribbons they use for badges was all gone and Joe looked so sorry, he said he wanted to take a piece of ribbon home to let his wife know that he belonged to the Reform Club, Miss Gordon heard him, and she had a piece of black lace and red ribbon twisted together around her throat and she separated the lace from the ribbon and tied it in his button-hole, so his Mary would see it. Oh Miss Belle did look so sweet and Mr. Clifford never took his eyes off her. I think he admires her very much."

"I don't see how he can help it, she is one of the dearest—sweetest, ladies I ever saw, she never seemed to say by her actions, 'I am doing so much for you poor people' and you can't be too thankful."

"Not she, and between you and I, and the gate-post, I think that will be a match."

"I think it would make a splendid one, but hush, I hear some persons coming."

The door opened and Paul Clifford, Joe Gough, and Belle Gordon entered.

"Here Mrs. Gough," said Paul Clifford, "as we children used to say. Here's your husband safe and sound, and I will add, a member of our reformed club and we have come to congratulate you upon the event."

"My dear friends, I am very thankful to you for your great kindness, I don't think I shall ever be able to repay you."

"Don't be uneasy darling," said Belle, "we are getting our pay as we go along, we don't think the cause of humanity owes us anything."

"Yes," said Joe seating himself by the bed side with an air of intense gratification. "Here is my badge, I did not want to leave the meeting without having this to show you."

"This evening," said Mrs. Gough smiling through her tears, "reminds me of a little temperance song I learned when a child, I think it commenced with these words:

> *"And are you sure the news is true?*
> *Are you sure my John has joined?*
> *I can't believe the happy news,*
> *And leave my fears behind,*
> *If John has joined and drinks no more,*
> *The happiest wife am I*
> *That ever swept a cabin floor,*
> *Or sung a lullaby.*

"That's just the way I feel to-night, I haven't been so happy before for years."

"And I hope," said Mr. Clifford, "that you will have many happy days and nights in the future."

"And I hope so too," said Joe, shaking hands with Paul and Belle as they rose to go.

Mr. Clifford accompanied Belle to her door, and as they parted she said, "This is a glorious work in which it is our privilege to clasp hands."

"It is and I hope," but as the words rose to his lips, he looked into the face of Belle, and it was so radiant with intelligent tenderness and joy, that she seemed to him almost like a glorified saint, a being too precious high and good for common household uses, and so the remainder of the sentence died upon his lips and he held his peace.

# XV

I have resolved to dissolve partnership with Charles," said Augustine Romaine to his wife, the next morning after his son's return from the Champaign supper at John Anderson's.

"Oh! no you are not in earnest, are you? You seem suddenly to have lost all patience with Charlie."

"Yes I have, and I have made up my mind that I am not going to let him hang like a millstone on our business. No, if he will go down, I am determined he shall not drag me down with him. See what a hurt it would be to us, to have it said, 'Don't trust your case with the Romaine's for the Junior member of that firm is a confirmed drunkard.'"

"Well, Augustine you ought to know best, but it seems like casting him off, to dissolve partnership with him."

"I can't help it, if he persists in his downward course he must take the consequences. Charles has had every advantage; when other young lawyers have had to battle year after year with obscurity and poverty, he entered into a business that was already established and flourishing. What other men were struggling for, he found ready made to his hand, and if he chooses to throw away every advantage and make a complete wreck of himself, I can't help it."

"Oh! it does seem so dreadful, I wonder what will become of my poor boy?"

"Now, mother I want you to look at this thing in the light of reason and common sense. I am not turning Charles out of the house. He is not poor, though the way he is going on he will be. You know his grandfather has left him a large estate out West, which is constantly increasing in value. Now what I mean to do is to give Charles a chance to set up for himself as attorney, wherever he pleases. Throwing him on his own resources, with a sense of responsibility, may be the best thing for him; but in the present state of things I do not think it advisable to continue our business relations together. For more than twenty-five years our firm has stood foremost at the bar. Ever since my brother and I commenced business together our reputation has been unspotted and I mean to keep it so, if I have to cut off my right hand."

Mrs. Romaine gazed upon the stern sad face of her husband, and felt by the determination of his manner that it was useless to entreat or reason with him to change his purpose; and so with a heavy heart, and eyes drooping with unshed tears, she left the room.

"John," said Mr. Romaine to the waiter, "tell Charles I wish to see him before I go down to the office." Just then Charles entered the room and bade good morning to his father.

"Good morning," replied his father, rather coldly, and for a moment there was an awkward silence.

"Charles," said Mr. Romaine, "after having witnessed the scene of last night, I have come to the conclusion to dissolve the partnership between us."

"Just as you please," said Charles in a tone of cold indifference that irritated his father; but he maintained his self-control.

"I am sorry that you will persist in your downward course; but if you are determined to throw yourself away I have made up my mind to cut loose from you. I noticed last week when you were getting out the briefs in that Sumpter case, you were not yourself, and several times lately you have made me hang my head in the court room. I am sorry, very sorry," and a touch of deep emotion gave a tone of tenderness to the closing sentence. There was a slight huskiness in Charles' voice, as he replied, "Whenever the articles of dissolution are made out I am ready to sign."

"They shall be ready by to-morrow."

"All right, I will sign them."

"And what then?"

"Set up for myself, the world is wide enough for us both."

After Mr. Romaine had left the room, Charles sat, burying his head in his hands and indulging bitter thoughts toward his father. "To-day," he said to himself, "he resolved to cut loose from me apparently forgetting that it was from his hands, and at his table I received my first glass of wine. He prides himself on his power of self-control, and after all what does it amount to? It simply means this, that he has an iron constitution, and can drink five times as much as I can without showing its effects, and to-day if Mr. R.N. would ask him to sign the total-abstinence pledge, he wouldn't hear to it. Yes I am ready to sign any articles he will bring, even if it is to sign never to enter this house, or see his face; but my mother—poor mother, I am sorry for her sake."

Just then his mother entered the room.

"My son."

"Mother."

"Just what I feared has come to pass. I have dreaded more than anything else this collision with your father."

"Now mother don't be so serious about this matter. Father's law office does not take in the whole world. I shall either set up for myself in A.P., or go West."

"Oh! don't talk of going away, I think I should die of anxiety if you were away."

"Well, as I passed down the street yesterday I saw there was an office to let in Frazier's new block, and I think I will engage it and put out my sign. How will that suit you?"

"Anything, or anywhere, Charlie, so you are near me. And Charlie don't be too stout with your father, he was very much out of temper when you came home last night, but be calm; it will blow over in a few days, don't add fuel to the fire. And you know that you and Miss Roland are to be married in two weeks, and I do wish that things might remain as they are, at least till after the wedding. Separation just now might give rise to some very unpleasant talk, and I would rather if you and your father can put off this dissolution, that you will consent to let things remain as they are for a few weeks longer. When your father comes home I will put the case to him, and have the thing delayed. Just now Charles I dread the consequences of a separation."

"Well, Mother, just as you please; perhaps the publication of the articles of dissolution in the paper might complicate matters."

When Mr. Romaine returned home, his wrath was somewhat mollified, and Mrs. Romaine having taken care to prepare his favorite dishes for dinner, took the opportunity when he had dined to entreat him to delay the intended separation till after the wedding, to which he very graciously consented.

AGAIN THERE WAS A MERRY gathering at the home of Jeanette Roland. It was her wedding night, and she was about to clasp hands for life with Charles Romaine. True to her idea of taking things as she found them, she had consented to be his wife without demanding of him any reformation from the habit which was growing so fearfully upon him. His wealth and position in society like charity covered a multitude of sins. At times Jeanette felt misgivings about the step she was about to take, but she put back the thoughts like unwelcome intruders, and like the Ostrich, hiding her head in the sand, instead of avoiding the danger, she shut her eyes to its fearful reality. That night the wine flowed out like a purple flood; but the men and women who drank were people of culture, wealth and position, and did not seem to think it was just as disgraceful or more so to drink in excess in magnificently furnished parlors, as it was in low Barrooms or miserable dens where vice and poverty are huddled together. And if the weary children of hunger and hard toil instead of seeking sleep as nature's sweet restorer, sought to stimulate their flagging energies in the enticing cup, they with the advantages of wealth, culture and refinement could not plead the excuses of extreme wretchedness, or hard and unremitting drudgery.

"How beautiful, very beautiful," fell like a pleasant ripple upon the ear of Jeanette Roland, as she approached the altar, beneath her wreath of orange blossoms, while her bridal veil floated like a cloud of lovely mist from her fair young head. The vows were spoken, the bridal ring placed upon her finger, and amid a train of congratulating friends, she returned home where a sumptuous feast awaited them.

"Don't talk so loud, but I think Belle Gordon acted wisely when she refused Mr. Romaine," said Mrs. Gladstone, one of the guests.

"Do you, indeed? Why Charles Romaine, is the only son of Mr. Romaine, and besides being the heir he has lately received a large legacy from his grandfather's estate. I think Jeanette has made a splendid match. I hope my girls will do as well."

"I hope on the other hand that my girls will never marry unless they do better."

"Why how you talk! What's the matter with Mr. Romaine?"

"Look at him now," said Mrs. Fallard joining in the conversation. "This is his wedding night and yet you can plainly see he is under the influence of wine. Look at those eyes, don't you know how beautiful and clear they are when he is sober, and how very interesting he is in conversation. Now look at him, see how muddled his eye is—but he is approaching—listen to his utterance, don't you notice how thick it is? Now if on his wedding night, he can not abstain, I have very grave fears for Jeanette's future."

"Perhaps you are both right, but I never looked at things in that light before, and I know that a magnificent fortune can melt like snow in the hands of a drunken man."

"I wish you much joy," rang out a dozen voices, as Jeanette approached them. "Oh Jeanette, you just look splendid! and Mr. Romaine, oh he is so handsome." "Oh Jeanette what's to hinder you from being so happy?" "But where is Mr. Romaine? we have missed him for some time." "I don't know, let me seek my husband." "Isn't that a mouthful?" said Jeanette laughingly disengaging herself from the merry group, as an undefined sense of apprehension swept over her. Was it a presentiment of coming danger? An unspoken prophecy to be verified by bitter tears, and lonely fear that seemed for a moment to turn life's sweetness into bitterness and gall. In the midst of a noisy group, in the dining room, she found Charles drinking the wine as it gave its color aright in the cup. She saw the deep flush upon his cheek, and the cloudiness of his eye, and for the first time upon that bridal night she felt a shiver of fear as the veil was suddenly lifted before her unwilling eye; and half reluctantly she said to herself, "Suppose after all my cousin Belle was right."

# XVI

G ood morning! Mr. Clifford," said Joe Gough, entering the store of Paul Clifford, the next day after he joined the Reform Club. "I have heard that you wanted some one to help you, and I am ready to do anything to make an honest living."

"I am very sorry," said Paul, "but I have just engaged a young man belonging to our Club to come this morning."

Joe looked sad, but not discouraged, and said, "Mr. Clifford, I want to turn over a new leaf in my life, but everyone does not know that. Do you know of any situation I can get? I have been a book-keeper and a salesman in the town of C., where I once lived, but I am willing to begin almost anywhere on the ladder of life, and make it a stepping-stone to something better."

There was a tone of earnestness in his voice, and an air of determination, in his manner that favorably impressed Paul Clifford and he replied,—

"I was thinking of a friend of mine who wants a helping hand; but it may not be, after all, the kind of work you prefer. He wants a porter, but as you say you want to make your position a stepping-stone to something better, if you make up your mind to do your level best, the way may open before you in some more congenial and unexpected quarter. Wait a few minutes, and I will give you a line to him. No! I can do better than that; he is a member of our Club, and I will see him myself; but before you do, had we better not go to the barber's?"

"I would like to," said Joe, "but I haven't—"

"Haven't the money?"

"Yes, Mr. Clifford, that's the fact, I am not able to pay even for a shave. Oh! what a fool I have been."

"Oh! well never mind, let the dead past, bury its dead. The future is before you, try and redeem that. If you accept it, I will lend you a few dollars. I believe in lending a helping hand. So come with me to the barber's and I'll make it all right, you can pay me when you are able, but here we are at the door, let us go in."

They entered, and in a few moments Joe's face was under the manipulating care of the barber.

"Fix this so," said Joe to the barber, giving him directions how to cut his mustache.

Paul was somewhat amused, and yet in that simple act, he saw a return of self-respect, and was glad to see its slightest manifestations, and it was pleasant to witness the satisfaction with which Joe beheld himself in the glass, as he exclaimed, "Why Mary would hardly know me!"

"Suppose now, we go to the tailor's and get some new rigging?"

"Mr. Clifford," said Joe hesitatingly, "you are very kind, but I don't know when I shall be able to pay you, and—"

"Oh! never mind, when you are able I will send my bill. It will help you in looking for a place to go decently dressed. So let us go into the store and get a new suit."

They entered a clothing store and in a few moments Joe was dressed in a new suit which made him look almost like another person.

"Now, we are ready," said Paul, "appearances are not so much against you."

"Good morning Mr. Tennant," said Paul to the proprietor of a large store. "I heard last night that you wanted help in your store and I have brought you Mr. Gough, who is willing to take any situation you will give him, and I will add, he is a member of our Reform Club."

Mr. Tennant looked thoughtfully a moment, and replied, "I have only one vacancy, and I do not think it would suit your friend. My porter died yesterday and that is the only situation which I can offer him at present."

"I will accept it," said Joe, "if you will give it to me, I am willing to do anything to make an honest living for my family."

"Well you can come to-morrow, or stop now and begin."

"All right," said Joe with a promptness that pleased his employer, and Joe was installed in the first day's regular work he had had for months.

"What! sitting up sewing?" said Belle Gordon entering the neat room where Mrs. Gough was rejuvenating a dress for her older daughter. "Why you look like another woman, your cheeks are getting plump, your eyes are brightening, and you look so happy."

"I feel just like I look, Miss Gordon. Joe has grown so steady, he gets constant work, and he is providing so well for us all, and he won't hear to me taking again that slop-shop work. He says all he wants me to do, is to get well, and take care of the home and children. But you look rather pale, have you been sick?"

"Yes, I have been rather unwell for several weeks, and the doctor has ordered among other things that I should have a plentiful supply of fresh air, so to-morrow as there is to be a free excursion, and I am on the Committee, I think if nothing prevents, I shall go. Perhaps you would like to go?"

"Yes, if Joe will consent, but—"

"But, what?"

"Well Joe has pretty high notions, and I think he may object, because it is receiving charity. I can't blame him for it, but Joe has a right smart of pride that way."

"No! I don't blame him, I rather admire his spirit of self-reliance, and I wouldn't lay the weight of my smallest finger upon his self-respect to repress it; still I would like to see your Mamy, and Hatty, have a chance to get out into the woods, and have what I call a good time. I think I can have it so arranged that you can go with me, and serve as one of the Committee on refreshments, and your services would be an ample compensation for your entertainment."

"Well if you put it in that light, I think Joe would be willing for me to go."

"I will leave the matter there, and when your husband comes home you can consult him and send me word. And so you are getting along nicely?"

"Oh! yes indeed, splendidly. Just look here, this is Joe's present," and Mary held up with both hands a beautifully embossed and illustrated Bible. "This was my birth-day present. Oh! Miss Belle, Joe seems to me like another man. Last night we went to a conference and prayer-meeting, and Joe spoke. Did you know he had joined the church?"

"No! when did that happen?"

"Last week."

"Has he become religious?"

"Well I think Joe's trying to do the best he can. He said last night in meeting that he felt like a new man, and if they didn't believe he had religion to ask his wife."

"And suppose they had asked you, what would you have said?"

"I would have said I believe Joe's a changed man, and I hope he will hold out faithful. And Miss Belle I want to be a Christian, but there are some things about religion I can't understand. People often used to talk to me about getting religion, and getting ready to die. Religion somehow got associated in my mind with sorrow and death, but it seems to me since I have known you and Mr. Clifford the thing looks different. I got it associated with something else besides the pall, the hearse, and weeping mourners. You have made me feel that it is as beautiful and valuable for life as it is necessary for death. And yet there are some things I can't understand. Miss Belle will you be shocked if I tell you something which has often puzzled me?"

"I don't know, I hope you have nothing very shocking to tell me."

"Well perhaps it is, and maybe I had better not say it."

"But you have raised my curiosity, and woman like I want to hear it."

"Now don't be shocked, but let me ask you, if you really believe that God is good?"

"Yes I do, and to doubt it would be to unmoor my soul from love, from peace, and rest. It seems to me to believe that must be the first resting place for my soul, and I feel that with me

> *"To doubt would be disloyalty*
> *To falter would be sin.*

"But my dear I have been puzzled just as you have, and can say,—

> *"I have wandered in mazes dark and distressing*
> *I've had not a cheering ray my spirit to bless,*
> *Cheerless unbelief held my laboring soul in grief."*

"And what then?"

> *"I then turned to the Gospel that taught me to pray*
> *And trust in the living word from folly away.*

"And it was here my spirit found a resting place, and I feel that in believing I have entered into rest."

"Ah!" said Mary to herself when Belle was gone, "there is something so restful and yet inspiring in her words. I wish I had her faith."

# XVII

I am sorry, very sorry," said Belle Gordon, as a shadow of deep distress flitted over her pale sad face. She was usually cheerful and serene in her manner; but now it seemed as if the very depths of her soul had been stirred by some mournful and bitter memory. "Your question was so unexpected and—"

"And what!" said Paul in a tone of sad expectancy, "so unwelcome?"

"It was so sudden, I was not prepared for it."

"I do not," said Paul, "ask an immediate reply. Give yourself ample time for consideration."

"Mr. Clifford," said Belle, her voice gathering firmness as she proceeded, "while all the relations of life demand that there should be entire truthfulness between us and our fellow creatures, I think we should be especially sincere and candid in our dealings with each other on this question of marriage, a question not only as affecting our own welfare but that of others, a relation which may throw its sunshine or shadow over the track of unborn ages. Permit me now to say to you, that there is no gentleman of my acquaintance whom I esteem more highly than yourself; but when you ask me for my heart and hand, I almost feel as if I had no heart to give; and you know it would be wrong to give my hand where I could not place my heart."

"But would it be impossible for you to return my affection?" "I don't know, but I am only living out my (vow) of truthfulness when I say to you, I feel as if I had been undone for love. You tell that in offering your hand that you bring me a heart unhackneyed in the arts of love, that my heart is the first and only shrine on which you have ever laid the wealth of your affections. I cannot say the same in reply. I have had my bright and beautiful day dream, but it has faded, and I have learned what is the hardest of all lessons for a woman to learn. I have learned to live without love."

"Oh no," said Paul, "not to live without love. In darkened homes how many grateful hearts rejoice to hear your footsteps on the threshold. I have seen the eyes of young Arabs of the street grow brighter as you approached and say, 'That's my lady, she comes to see my mam when she's sick.' And I have seen little girls in the street quicken their face to catch a loving smile from their dear Sunday school teacher. Oh Miss Belle instead of living without love, I think you are surrounded with a cordon of loving hearts."

"Yes, and I appreciate them—but this is not the love to which I refer. I mean a love which is mine, as anything else on earth is mine, a love precious, enduring and strong, which brings hope and joy and sunshine over one's path in life. A love which commands my allegiance and demands my respect. This is the love I have learned to do without, and perhaps the poor and needy had learned to love me less, had this love surrounded me more."

"Miss Belle, perhaps I was presumptuous, to have asked a return of the earnest affection I have for you; but I had hoped that you would give the question some consideration; and may I not hope that you will think kindly of my proposal? Oh Miss Gordon, ever since the death of my sainted mother, I have had in my mind's eye the ideal of a woman nobly planned, beautiful, intellectual, true and affectionate, and you have filled out that ideal in all its loveliest proportions, and I hope that my desire will not be like reaching out to some bright particular star and wishing to win it. It seems to me," he said with increasing earnestness, "whatever obstacle may be in the way, I would go through fire and water to remove it."

"I am sorry," said Belle as if speaking to herself, and her face had an absent look about it, as if instead of being interested in the living present she was grouping amid the ashes of the dead past. At length she said, "Mr. Clifford, permit me to say in the first place, let there be truth between us. If my heart seems callous and indifferent to your love, believe me it is warm to esteem and value you as a friend, I might almost say as a brother, for in sympathy of feeling and congeniality of disposition you are nearer to me than my own brother; but I do not think were I so inclined that it would be advisable for me to accept your hand without letting you know something of my past history. I told you a few moments since that I had my day dream. Permit me to tell you, for I think you are entitled to my confidence. The object of that day dream was Charles Romaine."

"Charles Romaine!" and there was a tone of wonder in the voice, and a puzzled look on the face of Paul Clifford.

"Yes! Charles Romaine, not as you know him now, with the marks of dissipation on his once handsome face, but Charles Romaine, as I knew him when he stood upon the threshold of early manhood, the very incarnation of beauty, strength and grace. Not Charles Romaine with the blurred and bloated countenance, the staggering gait, the confused and vacant eye; but Charles Romaine as a young, handsome and talented lawyer, the pride of our village, the hope of his father and the joy of his mother; before whom the future was opening full of rich and rare promises. Need I tell you that when he sought my hand in preference to all the other girls in our village, that I gave him what I never can give to another, the first, deep love of my girlish heart. For nearly a whole year I wore his betrothal ring upon my finger, when I saw to my utter anguish and dismay that he was fast becoming a drunkard. Oh! Mr. Clifford if I could have saved him I would have taken blood from every vein and strength from every nerve. We met frequently at entertainments. I noticed time after time, the effects of the wine he had imbibed, upon his manner and conversation. At first I shrank from remonstrating with him, until the burden lay so heavy on my heart that I felt I must speak out, let the consequences be what they might. And so one evening I told him plainly and seriously my fears about his future. He laughed lightly and said my fears were unfounded; that I was nervous and giving away to idle fancies; that his father always had wine at the table, and that he had never seen him under the influence of liquor. Silenced, but not convinced, I watched his course with painful solicitude. All remonstrances on my part seemed thrown away; he always had the precedent of his father to plead in reply to my earnest entreaties. At last when remonstrances and entreaties seemed to be all in vain, I resolved to break the engagement. It may have been a harsh and hard alternative, but I would not give my hand where my respect could not follow. It may be that I thought too much of my own happiness, but I felt that marriage must be for me positive misery or positive happiness, and I feared that if I married a man so lacking in self-control as to become a common drunkard, that when I ceased to love and respect him, I should be constantly tempted to hate and despise him. I think one of the saddest fates that can befall a woman is to be tied for life to a miserable bloated wreck of humanity. There may be some women with broad generous hearts, and great charity, strong enough to lift such men out of the depths, but I had no such faith in my strength and so I gave him back his ring. He accepted it, but we parted as friends. For awhile after our engagement was broken, we occasionally met at the houses of our mutual friends in social gatherings and I noticed with intense satisfaction that whenever wine was offered he scrupulously abstained from ever tasting a drop, though I think at times his self-control was severely tested. Oh! what hope revived in my heart. Here

FRANCES ELLEN WATKINS HARPER

I said to myself is compensation for all I have suffered, if by it he shall be restored to manhood usefulness and society, and learn to make his life not a thing of careless ease and sensuous indulgence, but of noble struggle and high and holy endeavor. But while I was picturing out for him a magnificent future, imagining the lofty triumphs of his intellect—an intellect grand in its achievements and glorious in its possibilities, my beautiful daydream was rudely broken up, and vanished away like the rays of sunset mingling with the shadows of night. My Aunt Mrs. Roland, celebrated her silver-wedding and my cousin's birth-day by giving a large entertainment; and among other things she had a plentiful supply of wine. Mr. Romaine had lately made the acquaintance of my cousin Jeanette Roland. She was both beautiful in person and fascinating in her manners, and thoughtlessly she held a glass of wine in her hand and asked Mr. Romaine if he would not honor the occasion, by drinking her mother's health. For a moment he hesitated, his cheek paled and flushed alternately, he looked irresolute. While I watched him in silent anguish it seemed as if the agony of years was compressed in a few moments. I tried to catch his eye but failed, and with a slight tremor in his hand he lifted the glass to his lips and drank. I do not think I would have felt greater anguish had I seen him suddenly drowned in sight of land. Oh! Mr. Clifford that night comes before me so vividly, it seems as if I am living it all over again. I do not think Mr. Romaine has ever recovered from the reawakening of his appetite. He has since married Jeanette. I meet her occasionally. She has a beautiful home, dresses magnificently, and has a retinue of servants; and yet I fancy she is not happy. That somewhere hidden out of sight there is a worm eating at the core of her life. She has a way of dropping her eyes and an absent look about her that I do not fully understand, but it seems to me that I miss the old elasticity of her spirits, the merry ring of her voice, the pleasant thrills of girlish laughter, and though she never confesses it to me I doubt that Jeanette is happy. And with this sad experience in the past can you blame me if I am slow, very slow to let the broken tendrils of my heart entwine again?"

"Miss Belle," said Paul Clifford catching eagerly at the smallest straw of hope, "if you can not give me the first love of a fresh young life, I am content with the rich aftermath of your maturer years, and ask from life no higher prize; may I not hope for that?"

"I will think on it but for the present let us change the subject."

"Do you think Jeanette is happy? She seems so different from what she used to be," said Miss Tabitha Jones to several friends who were spending the evening with her.

"Happy!" replied Mary Gladstone, "don't see what's to hinder her from being happy. She has everything that heart can wish. I was down to her house yesterday, and she has just moved in her new home. It has all the modern improvements, and everything is in excellent taste. Her furniture is of the latest style, and I think it is really superb."

"Yes," said her sister, "and she dresses magnificently. Last week she showed me a most beautiful set of jewelry, and a camel's hair shawl, and I believe it is real camel's hair. I think you could almost run it through a ring. If I had all she has, I think I should be as happy as the days are long. I don't believe I would let a wave of trouble roll across my peaceful breast."

"Oh! Annette," said Mrs. Gladstone, "don't speak so extravagantly, and I don't like to hear you quote those lines for such an occasion."

"Why not mother? Where's the harm?"

"That hymn has been associated in my mind with my earliest religious impressions and experience, and I don't like to see you lift it out of its sacred associations, for such a trifling occasion."

"Oh mother you are so strict. I shall never be able to keep time with you, but I do think, if I was off as Jeanette, that I would be as blithe and happy as a lark, and instead of that she seems to be constantly drooping and fading."

"Annette," said Mrs. Gladstone, "I knew a woman who possesses more than Jeanette does, and yet she died of starvation."

"Died of starvation! Why, when, and where did that happen? and what became of her husband?"

"He is in society, caressed and ed on by the young girls of his set and I have seen a number of managing mammas to whom I have imagined he would not be an objectionable son-in-law."

"Do I know him mother?"

"No! and I hope you never will."

"Well mother I would like to know how he starved his wife to death and yet escaped the law."

"The law helped him."

"Oh mother!" said both girls opening their eyes in genuine astonishment.

"I thought," said Mary Gladstone, "it was the province of the law to protect women, I was just telling Miss Basanquet yesterday, when she was talking about woman's suffrage that I had as many rights as I wanted and that I was willing to let my father and brothers do all the voting for me."

"Forgetting my dear, that there are millions of women who haven't such fathers and brothers as you have. No my dear, when you examine the matter, a little more closely, you will find there are some painful inequalities in the law for women."

"But mother, I do think it would be a dreadful thing for women to vote Oh! just think of women being hustled and crowded at the polls by rude men, their breaths reeking with whiskey and tobacco, the very air heavy with their oaths. And then they have the polls at public houses. Oh mother, I never want to see the day when women vote."

"Well I do, because we have one of the kindest and best fathers and husbands and good brothers, who would not permit the winds of heaven to visit us too roughly, there is no reason we should throw ourselves between the sunshine and our less fortunate sisters who shiver in the blast."

"But mother, I don't see how voting would help us, I am sure we have influence I have often heard papa say that you were the first to awaken him to a sense of the enormity of slavery. Now mother if we women would use our influence with our fathers, brothers, husbands, and sons, could we not have everything we want."

"No, my dear we could not, with all our influence we never could have the same sense of responsibility which flows from the possession of power. I want women to possess power as well as influence, I want every Christian woman as she passes by a grogshop or liquor saloon, to feel that she has on her heart a burden of responsibility for its existence, I hold my dear that a nation as well as an individual should have a conscience, and on this liquor question there is room for woman's conscience not merely as a persuasive influence but as an enlightened and aggressive power."

"Well Ma I think you would make a first class stump speaker. I expect when women vote we shall be constantly having calls, for the gifted, and talented Mrs. Gladstone to speak on the duties and perils of the hour."

"And I would do it, I would go among my sister women and try to persuade them to use their vote as a moral lever, not to make home less happy, but society more holy. I would have good and sensible women, grave in manner, and cultured in intellect, attend the primary meetings and bring their moral influence and political power to frown down corruption, chicanery, and low cunning."

"But mother just think if women went to the polls how many vicious ones would go?"

"I hope and believe for the honor of our sex that the vicious women of the community are never in the majority, that for one woman whose feet turn aside from the paths of rectitude that there are thousands of feet that never stray into forbidden paths, and today I believe there is virtue enough in society to confront its vice, and intelligence enough to grapple with its ignorance."

# XVIII

"Why Mrs. Gladstone," said Miss Tabitha, "you are as zealous as a new convert to the cause of woman suffrage. We single women who are constantly taxed without being represented, know what it is to see ignorance and corruption striking hands together and voting away our money for whatever purposes they choose. I pay as large a tax as many of the men in A.P., and yet cannot say who shall assess my property for a single year."

"And there is another thing," said Mrs. Gladstone, "ought to be brought to the consideration of the men, and it is this. They refuse to let us vote and yet fail to protect our homes from the ravages of rum. My young friend, whom I said died of starvation; foolishly married a dissipated man who happened to be rich and handsome. She was gentle, loving, sensitive to a fault. He was querulous, fault-finding and irritable, because his nervous system was constantly unstrung by liquor. She lacked tenderness, sympathy and heart support, and at last faded and died, not starvation of the body, but a trophy of the soul, and when I say the law helped, I mean it licensed the places that kept the temptation ever in his way. And I fear, that is the secret of Jeanette's faded looks, and unhappy bearing."

No Jeanette was not happy. Night after night would she pace the floor of her splendidly furnished chamber waiting and watching for her husband's footsteps. She and his friends had hoped that her influence would be strong enough to win him away from his boon companions, that his home and beautiful bride would present superior attractions to Anderson's saloon, his gambling pool, and champaign suppers, and for a while they did, but soon the novelty wore off, and Jeanette found out to her great grief that her power to bind him to the simple attractions of home were as futile as a role of cobwebs to moor a ship to the shore, when it has drifted out and is dashing among the breakers. He had learned to live an element of excitement, and to depend upon artificial stimulation, until it seemed as if the very blood in his veins grew sluggish fictitious excitement was removed. His father, hopeless of his future, had dissolved partnership with him, and for months there had been no communication between them; and Jeanette saw with agony and dismay that his life was being wrecked upon the broad sea of sin and shame.

"WHERE IS HIS FATHER? THE child can't live. It is one of the worst cases of croup I have had this year, why didn't you send for me sooner? Where is his father? It is now just twelve o'clock, time for all respectable men to be in the house," said the bluff but kind hearted family doctor looking tenderly upon Jeanette's little boy who lay gasping for breath in the last stages of croup.

"Oh! I don't know," said Jeanette her face crimsoning beneath the doctor's searching glance. "I suppose he is down to Anderson's."

"Anderson's!" said the doctor in a tone of hearty indignation, "what business has he there, and his child dying here?"

"But doctor, he didn't know, the child had fever when he went out, but neither of us thought much of it till I was awakened by his strange and unnatural breathing. I sent for you as soon as I could rouse the servants." "Well rouse them again, and tell them to go down to Anderson's and tell your husband that his child is dying."

"Oh! no not dying doctor, you surely don't mean it." "Yes Jeanette," said the old family doctor, tenderly and sadly, "I can do nothing for him, let me take him in my arms and rest you. Dear little darling, he will be saved from the evils to come."

Just as his life was trembling on its frailest chords, and its delicate machinery almost wound up, Charles Romaine returned, sober enough to take in the situation. He strode up to the dying child, took the clammy hands in his, and said in a tone of bitter anguish, "Charlie, don't you know papa? Wouldn't you speak one little word to papa?" But it was too late, the shadows that never deceive flitted over the pale beauty of the marble brow, the waxen lid closed over the once bright and laughing eye, and the cold grave for its rest had won the child.

# XIX

(Text missing.)

# XX

If riches could bring happiness, John Anderson should be a happy man; and yet he is far from being happy. He has succeeded in making money, but failed in every thing else. But let us enter his home. As you open the parlor door your feet sink in the rich and beautiful carpet. Exquisite statuary, and superbly framed pictures greet your eye and you are ready to exclaim, "Oh! how lovely." Here are the beautiful conceptions of painters' art and sculptors' skill. It is a home of wealth, luxury and display, but not of love, refinement and culture. Years since, before John Anderson came to live in the city of A.P. he had formed an attachment for an excellent young lady who taught school in his native village, and they were engaged to be married; but after coming to the city and forming new associations, visions of wealth dazzled his brain, and unsettled his mind, till the idea of love in a cottage grew distasteful to him. He had seen men with no more ability than himself who had come to the city almost pennyless, and who had grown rich in a few years, and he made up his mind that if possible he would do two things, acquire wealth and live an easy life, and he thought the easiest way to accomplish both ends was to open up a gorgeous palace of sin and entice into his meshes the unwary, the inexperienced, and the misguided slaves of appetite. For awhile after he left his native village, he wrote almost constantly to his betrothed; but as new objects and interests engaged his attention, his letters became colder and less frequent, until they finally ceased and the engagement was broken. At first the blow fell heavily upon the heart of his affianced, but she was too sensible to fade away and die the victim of unrequited love, and in after years when she had thrown her whole soul into the temperance cause, and consecrated her life to the work of uplifting fallen humanity, she learned to be thankful that it was not her lot to be united to a man who stood as a barrier across the path of human progress and would have been a weight to her instead of wings. Released from his engagement, he entered into an alliance (for that is the better name for a marriage) which was not a union of hearts, or intercommunion of kindred souls; but only an affair of convenience; in a word he married for money a woman, who was no longer young in years, nor beautiful in person, nor amiable in temper. But she was rich, and her money like charity covered a multitude of faults, and as soon as he saw the golden bait he caught at it, and they were married, for he was willing to do almost any thing for money, except work hard for it. It was a marriage however that brought no happiness to either party. Mrs. Anderson was an illy educated, self willed, narrow minded (woman), full of airs and pretensions, the only daughter of a man who had laid the foundation of his wealth by keeping a low groggery, and dying had left her his only heir. John Anderson was selfish and grasping. He loved money, and she loved display, and their home was often the scene of the most pitiful contentions about money matters. Harsh words and bitter recriminations were almost common household usages. The children brought up in this unhealthy atmosphere naturally took sides with their mother and their home was literally a house divided against itself. The foolish conduct of the mother inspired the children with disrespect for their father, who failed to support the authority of his wife as the mother and mistress of the home. As her sons grew older they often sought attractions in questionable places, away from the sombre influences of their fireside, and the daughters as soon as they stood upon the verge of early womanhood learned to look upon marriage as an escape valve from domestic discomforts; and in that beautiful home with all its costly surroundings, and sumptuous furniture, there was always something wanting, there was always a lack of tenderness, sympathy and mutual esteem.

"I can't afford it," said John Anderson, to his wife who had been asking for money for a trip to a fashionable watering place. "You will have to spend the summer elsewhere."

"Can't afford it! What nonsense; is not it as much to your interest as mine to carry the girls around and give them a chance?"

"A chance for what?"

"Why to see something of the world. You don't know what may happen. That English Earl was very attentive last night to Sophronia at Mrs. Jessap's ball."

"An English Count? who is he? and where did he spring from?"

"Why he's from England, and is said to be the only son and heir of a very rich nobleman."

"I don't believe it, I don't believe he is an Earl any more than I am."

"That's just like you, always throw cold water on every thing I say"

"It is no such thing, but I don't believe in picking up strangers and putting them into my bosom; it is not all gold that glitters."

"I know that, but how soon can you let me have some money? I want to go out this afternoon and do some shopping and engage the semptress."

"I tell you, Annette, I have not the money to spare; the money market is very tight, and I have very heavy bills to meet this month."

"The money market tight! why it has been tight ever since I have been married."

"Well you may believe it or not, just as you choose, but I tell you this crusading has made quite a hole in my business."

"Now John Anderson, tell that to somebody that don't know. I don't believe this crusading has laid a finger's weight upon your business."

"Yes it has, and if you read the papers you would find that it has even affected the revenue of the state and you will have to retrench somewhere."

"Well, I'll retrench somewhere. I think we are paying our servants too high wages any how. Mrs. Shenflint gets twice as much work done for the same money. I'll retrench, John Anderson, but I want you to remember that I did not marry you empty handed."

"I don't think I shall be apt to forget it in a hurry while I have such a gentle reminder at hand," he replied sarcastically.

"And I suppose you would not have married me if I had had no money."

"No, I would not," said John Anderson thoroughly exasperated, "and I would have been a fool if I had."

These bitter words spoken in a heat of passion were calculated to work disastrously in that sin darkened home.

For some time she had been suspecting that her money had been the chief inducement which led him to seek her hand, and now her worse suspicions were confirmed, and the last thread of confidence was severed.

"I should not have said it," said Anderson to himself, "but the woman is so provoking and unreasonable. I suppose she will have a fit of sulks for a month and never be done brooding over those foolish words"; and Anderson sighed as if he were an ill used man. He had married for money, and he had got what he bargained for; love, confidence, and mutual esteem were not sought in the contract and these do not necessarily come of themselves.

"Well, the best I can do is to give her what money she wants and be done with it."

"Is not in her room?"

"No sir and her bed has not been rumpled."

"Where in the world can she be?"

"I don't know, but here is a note she left."

"What does she say? read it Annette."

"She says she feels that you were unjust to the Earl and that she hopes you will forgive her the steps she has taken, but by the time the letter reaches you she expects to be the Countess of Clarendon."

"Poor foolish girl, you see what comes of taking a stranger to your bosom and making so much of him."

"That's just like you, John Anderson, every thing that goes wrong is blamed on me. I almost wish I was dead."

"I wish so too," thought Anderson but he concluded it was prudent to keep the wish to himself.

John Anderson had no faith whatever in the pretensions of his new son-in-law, but his vain and foolish wife on the other hand was elated at the dazzling prospects of her daughter, and often in her imagination visited the palatial residence of "My Son, the Earl," and was graciously received in society as the mother of the Countess of Clarendon. She was also highly gratified at the supposed effect of Sophronia's marriage upon a certain clique who had been too exclusive to admit her in their set. Should not those Gladstone girls be ready to snag themselves? and there was that Mary Talbot, did every thing she could to attract his attention but it was no go. My little Sophronia came along and took the rag off the bush. I guess they will almost die with envy. If he had waited for her father's consent we might have waited till the end of the chapter; but I took the responsibility on my shoulders and the thing is done. My daughter, the Countess of Clarendon. I like the ring of the words; but dear me here's the morning mail, and a letter from the Countess, but what does it mean?"

"Come to me, I am in great trouble."

In quick response to the appeal Mrs. Anderson took the first train to New York and found her daughter in great distress. The "Earl" had been arrested for forgery and stealing, and darker suspicions were hinted against him. He had been a body servant to a nobleman who had been travelling for his health and who had died by a lonely farmhouse where he had gone for fresh air and quiet, and his servant had seized upon his effects and letters of introduction, and passed himself off as the original Earl, and imitating his handwriting had obtained large remittances, for which he was arrested, tried and sent to prison, and thus ended the enchanting dream of "My daughter the Countess of Clarendon."

# XXI

I cannot ensure your life a single hour, unless you quit business. You are liable to be stricken with paralysis at any moment, if once subject to the (least) excitement. Can't you trust your business in the hands of your sons?"

"Doctor," said John Anderson, "I have only two boys. My oldest went West several years ago, and never writes to us unless he wants something, and as to Frank, if I would put the concern into his hands, he would drink himself into the grave in less than a month. The whole fact is this, my children are the curse of my life," and there was bitterness in the tone of John Anderson as he uttered these words of fearful sorrow.

"Well," said the doctor, "you must have rest and quiet or I will not answer for the consequences."

"Rest and quiet!" said John Anderson to himself, "I don't see how I am to get it, with such a wife as I have always worrying and bothering me about something." "Mr. Anderson," said one of the servants, "Mrs. Anderson says please come, as quick as possible into Mr. Frank's room."

"What's the matter now!"

"I don't know, but Mr. Frank's acting mightily queer; he thinks there are snakes and lizards crawling over him."

"He's got the horrors, just what I expected. Tell me about rest and quiet! I'll be there in a minute. Oh what's the matter? I feel strange," said Anderson falling back on the bed suddenly stricken with paralysis. While in another room lay his younger son a victim to delirium tremens, and dying in fearful agony. The curse that John Anderson had sent to other homes had come back darkened with the shadow of death to brood over his own habitation. His son is dying, but he has no word of hope to cheer the parting spirit as it passed out into the eternity, for him the darkness of the tomb, is not gilded with the glory of the resurrection.

The best medical skill has been summoned to the aid of John Anderson, but neither art, nor skill can bind anew the broken threads of life. The chamber in which he is confined is a marvel of decoration, light streams into his home through panes of beautifully stained glass. Pillows of the softest down are placed beneath his head, beautiful cushions lie at his feet that will never take another step on the errands of sin, but no appliances of wealth can give peace to his guilty conscience.

He looks back upon the past and the retrospect is a worse than wasted life; and when the future looms up before him he shrinks back from the contemplation, for the sins of the past throw their shadow over the future. He has houses, money and land, but he is a pauper in his soul, and a bankrupt in his character. In his eager selfish grasp for gold, he has shriveled his intellect and hardened and dried up his heart, and in so doing he has cut himself off from the richest sources of human enjoyment. He has wasted life's best opportunities, and there never was an angel, however bright, terrible and strong, that ever had power to roll away the stone from the grave of a dead opportunity, and what John Anderson has lost in time, he can never make up in eternity. He has formed no taste for reading, and thus has cut himself off from the glorious companionship of the good, the great, and the wise of all ages. He has been selfish, mean and grasping, and the blessing of the poor and needy never fall as benedictions on his weary head; and in that beautiful home with disease and death clutching at his heartstrings, he has wealth that he cannot enjoy, luxuries that pall upon his taste, and magnificence that can never satisfy the restless craving of his soul. His life has been a wretched failure. He neglected his children to amass the ways of iniquity, and their coldness and indifference pierce him like poisoned arrows. Marriage has brought him money, but not the sweet, tender ministrations of loving wifely care, and so he lives on starving in the midst of plenty; dying of thirst, with life's sweetest fountains eluding his grasp.

Charles Romaine is sleeping in a drunkard's grave. After the death of his boy there was a decided change in him. Night after night he tore himself away from John Anderson's saloon, and struggled with the monster that had enslaved him, and for awhile victory seemed to be perching on the banner of his resolution. Another child took the place of the first born, and the dead, and hope and joy began to blossom around Jeanette's path. His mother who had never ceased to visit the house marked the change with great satisfaction and prevailed upon his father to invite Charles and Jeanette to a New Year's dinner (only a family gathering). Jeanette being unwell excused herself from going, and Charles went alone. Jeanette felt a fearful foreboding when she saw him leaving the door, and said to herself, "I hope his father will not offer him wine. I am so afraid that something will happen to him, and yet I hated to persuade him not to go. His mother might think I was averse to his reconciliation with his father."

"It looks very natural to have Charles with us again," said Mrs. Ro(maine) looking fondly on her son.

"Yes, it seems like old times, when I always had my seat next to yours."

"And I hope," said his father, "it will never be vacant so long again."

The dinner hour passed on enlivened by social chat and pleasant reminiscences, and there was nothing to mar the harmony of the occasion. Mrs. Romaine had been careful to keep everything from the table that would be apt to awaken the old appetite for liquor, but after dinner Mr. Romaine invited Charles into the library to smoke. "Here," said he, handing him a cigar, "is one of the finest brands I have smoked lately, and by the way here is some rare old wine, more than 25 years old, which was sent to me yesterday by an old friend and college class mate of mine. Let me pour you out a glass." Charles suddenly became agitated, but as his father's back was turned to him, pouring out the wine, he did not notice the sudden paling of his cheek, and the hesitation of his manner. And Charles checking back his scruples took the glass and drained it, to the bottom.

There is a fable, that a certain king once permitted the devil to kiss his shoulder, and out of those shoulders sprang two serpents that in the fury of their hunger aimed at his head and tried to get at his brain. He tried to extricate himself from their terrible power. He tore at them with his fingers and found that it was his own flesh that he was lacerating. Dormant but not dead was the appetite for strong drink in Charles Romaine, and that one glass awakened the serpent coiled up in his flesh. He went out from his father's house with a newly awakened appetite clamoring and raging for strong drink. Every saloon he passed adding intensity to his craving. At last his appetite overmastered him and he almost rushed into a saloon, and waited impatiently till he was served. Every nerve seemed to be quivering with excitement, restlessness; and there was a look of wild despairing anguish on his face, as he clutched the glass to allay the terrible craving of his system. He drank till his head was giddy, and his gait was staggering, and then started for home. He entered the gate and slipped on the ice, and being too intoxicated to rise or comprehend his situation, he lay helpless in the dark and cold, until there crept over him that sleep from which there is no awakening, and when morning had broken in all its glory, Charles Romaine had drifted out of life, slain by the wine which at (last) had "bitten like an adder and stung like a serpent." Jeanette had waited and watched through the small hours of the night, till nature o'erwearied had sought repose in sleep and rising very early in the morning, she had gone to the front door to look down the street for his coming when the first object that met her gaze was the lifeless form of her husband. One wild and bitter shriek rent the air, and she fell fainting on the frozen corpse. Her friends gathered round her, all that love and tenderness could do was done for the wretched wife, but nothing could erase from her mind one agonizing sorrow, it was the memory of her fatal triumph over his good resolution years ago at her mother's silver wedding. Carelessly she had sowed the seeds of transgression whose fearful yield was a harvest of bitter misery. Mrs. Clifford came to her in her hour of trial, and tried to comfort and sustain the heart-stricken woman; who had tried to take life easy, but found it terribly hard, and she has measurably succeeded. In the home of her cousin she is trying to bear the burden of her life as well as she can. Her eye never lights up with joy. The bloom and flush have left her careworn face. Tears from her eyes long used to weeping have blenched the coloring of her life existence, and she is passing through life with the shadow of the grave upon her desolate heart.

Joe Gough has been true to his pledge, plenty and comfort have taken the place of poverty and pain. He continued his membership with the church of his choice and Mary is also striving to live a new life, and to be the ministering angel that keeps his steps, and he feels that in answer to prayer, his appetite for strong drink has been taken away.

Life with Mrs. Clifford has become a thing of brightness and beauty, and when children sprang up in her path making gladness and sunshine around her home, she was a wife and tender mother, fond but not foolish; firm in her household government, but not stern and unsympathising in her manner. The faithful friend and companion of her daughters, she won their confidence by her loving care and tender caution. She taught them to come to her in their hours of perplexity and trial and to keep no secrets from her sympathising heart. She taught her sons to be as upright in their lives and as pure in their conversation as she would have her daughters, recognizing for each only one code of morals and one law of spiritual life, and in course of time she saw her daughters ripening into such a beautiful womanhood, and her sons entering the arena of life not with the simplicity which is ignorant of danger and evil, but with the sterling integrity which baffles the darts of temptation with the panoply of principle and the armor of uprightness. Unconsciously she elevated the tone of society in which she moved by a life which was a beautiful and earnest expression of patient continuance in well doing. Paul Clifford's life has been a grand success, not in the mere accumulation of wealth, but in the enrichment of his moral and spiritual nature. He is still ever ready to lend a helping hand. He has not lived merely for wealth and enjoyment, but happiness, lasting and true springs up in his soul as naturally as a flower leaps into blossoms, and whether he is loved or hated, honored or forgotten, he constantly endeavors to make the world better by his example and gladdened by his presence feeling that if every one would be faithful to duty that even here, Eden would spring up in our path, and Paradise be around our way.

# A Note About the Author

Frances Ellen Watkins Harper (1825–1911) was an African American abolitionist, suffragist, poet, and novelist. Born free in Baltimore, Maryland, Harper became one of the first women of color to publish in the United States when her debut poetry collection *Forest Leaves* appeared in 1845. In 1850, she began to teach sewing at Union Seminary in Columbus, Ohio. The following year, alongside chairman of the Pennsylvania Abolition Society William Still, she began working as an abolitionist in earnest, helping slaves escape to Canada along the Underground Railroad. In 1854, having established herself as a prominent public speaker and political activist, Harper published *Poems on Miscellaneous Subjects*, a resounding critical and commercial success. Over the course of her life, Harper founded and participated in several progressive organizations, including the Women's Christian Temperance Union and the National Association of Colored Women. At the age of sixty-seven, Harper published *Iola Leroy, or Shadows Uplifted*, becoming one of the first African American women to publish a novel.

# A Note from the Publisher

Spanning many genres, from non-fiction essays to literature classics to children's books and lyric poetry, Mint Edition books showcase the master works of our time in a modern new package. The text is freshly typeset, is clean and easy to read, and features a new note about the author in each volume. Many books also include exclusive new introductory material. Every book boasts a striking new cover, which makes it as appropriate for collecting as it is for gift giving. Mint Edition books are only printed when a reader orders them, so natural resources are not wasted. We're proud that our books are never manufactured in excess and exist only in the exact quantity they need to be read and enjoyed.

# Discover more of your favorite classics with Bookfinity™.

- Track your reading with custom book lists.
- Get great book recommendations for your personalized Reader Type.
- Add reviews for your favorite books.
- AND MUCH MORE!

Visit **bookfinity.com** and take the fun Reader Type quiz to get started.

Enjoy our classic and modern companion pairings!